λ Magical Shift

Weres & Witches of Silver Lake
Book 1

Vella Day

Dedication

Without a doubt, this series would not exist without the help of my good friend, Carol Bezzo. I thank you from the bottom of my heart. And to the best beta reader—Tammy Thompson.

Beneath the calm and shimmering surface lie intrigue, power, magic, and danger.

Welcome to Silver Lake—where appearances can be deceiving, and what you see isn't truly what lies below.

Chapter One

OWEN CHANCELLOR COULDN'T believe his good luck. For the past few days, he had been stalking the beautiful Isadora Berta. Together with her long flowing red curls, creamy skin that had a light sprinkling of freckles, and deep blue eyes, she had enough sexy curves to make any man stop and stare.

This past hour, she'd traveled toward Westhaven, Scotland and then driven down a muddy dirt road, deep into the forest—alone. She then headed out on foot toward the cove bordering the North Sea, making her imminent capture a sure thing.

He couldn't wait to take this fair lass home to his family to be his wife. The fact that she hadn't even met him yet was a mere technicality. Once she saw him, she'd swoon as all the ladies did. He was taller than she was by a few inches, and his auburn hair and fair complexion would complement her looks rather well.

Loser indeed. He'd show his parents that he was worthy of their praise. Owen would train her to be a good and regal wife who would stand beside him at every occasion. He'd make sure she was honored by all.

He parked his four-wheel drive near hers, removed his clothes, and shifted into his wolf form to avoid leaving traces of his scattered clothes later on. He then scurried to the water's edge; it would be less obvious sneaking up on her as an animal. Once he spotted her, he slowly edged closer, hiding behind trees or the thick brush to make sure she couldn't see him. He then watched her prance around in her flowing white sundress. *Isadora, Isadora. Once you are mine, I'll have to teach you not to be so careless.*

Just as he was about to make his move, he noticed the strange marking on the back of her shoulder. The blue circle with a green vine growing through it was new to him, so very different from his red moon encased in a black circle. He had sensed she wasn't a shifter, but the intricate pattern must be a symbol for some group. But which one?

His future bride then bent down and lowered her hand to hover over the sand, and within seconds, a swirling cone erupted from the ground. Glancing upward, she giggled, the sound like small bells chiming. Despite her voice being light and airy, it wouldn't be appropriate for someone who was about to be a part of his prestigious clan. It was one more thing he'd have to change about her.

As she rose, the small force grew, and its sudden billowing size mesmerized him. How the hell was she doing that? As the cone of sand turned into a small twister, Isadora spun around and laughed. He'd never witnessed anyone with such powers. She had to be some kind of witch.

Fascinated and a bit unsettled by this new development, he decided not to capture her today; he needed to see the extent of her abilities. He didn't have long to wait. With the sand still spinning, she raised her arm and pointed toward the deep blue green sea as if commanding her creation to cut through the water. Dear goddess in heaven, the now rather massive sand storm actually parted the sea, cleaving it right down to the sandy bottom, and his respect for her grew significantly. This witch was far more than he had hoped.

With her calf-length dress hiked up to her knees, she walked into her self-made trough, the water never touching her. Owen blinked a few times wondering how this redheaded nymph had tricked him. She'd seemed rather ordinary before.

All of a sudden, she shot a ball of fire from her palm that bounced across the water, and he had to control himself to keep from howling. For a second, he was tempted to break cover and demand she tell him her secrets, but then reason intruded. His original scheme of capturing her in an effort to earn his rightful place in the family suddenly disintegrated. Joy surrounded him at the thought of what the two of them could accomplish together. To win her over though, he would have to resort to using his infinite charm.

Not wanting her spooked by a looming wolf, he decided it would be best if he left. Just as he turned around, she glanced over her shoulder in his direction, acting as if somehow he had disturbed her. While he couldn't be certain if she'd seen him or not, he quickly darted back up the path, excited at his new discovery. He wasn't sure how he'd accomplish his new goal, but one way or another Isadora Berta would become his.

IZZY HAD DONE it! For the past four years, she'd studied under the finest of her kind in Italy, France, and now, Scotland. Today was the first time she'd been able to literally part the sea. Not that her work was done by any means, but soon, she could return home and contribute to her family's safe keeping. Another two months of practicing, and her powers would be sharper than ever. Izzy's mentors had complimented her on her ability to control the wind, but her talent with fire definitely needed more work. One mistake could prove deadly, or at the very least, costly.

As she stood at the shoreline and admired the earth's beauty, a strange feeling of being watched washed over her again, but she shook it off. Several times this past week, she'd had the sense that someone was following her, but every time she looked over her shoulder, no one was there. It didn't really matter. It wasn't as if anyone could harm her.

With her tests complete, it was time to return to town. As she trekked back to her four-wheel drive Jeep, a strong vibration rattled her chest, causing her heart to pound and her body to shake. Recognizing the sensation, she stopped and waited for the imminent discussion from above.

"Izzy, your family needs you at home." The thought entered her conscious mind.

Family. Home. Her pulse tripped at the thought of what she'd given up to come here. She missed Silver Lake, Tennessee, but if she'd stayed, she never would have learned so much from the great witches of the world.

She hadn't heard from the moon goddess, Naliana, in over two years, and an unease spread through her at hearing those words. She looked up at the sky. *"May I ask why?"* she telepathed.

"No, my dear. Do as I say and return quickly, but let your arrival be a surprise."

Almost as soon as the tightening in her chest appeared, it was gone. One never disobeyed the moon goddess since she was the one who gave the Wendayans their powers in the first place. Izzy and her ancestors would have remained human with no powers had Naliana not interfered and bestowed magic to each of her kind.

A bit unsettled by the sudden command, Izzy hurried to her vehicle. As she was about to slip in, she spotted another set of tire tracks next to where she'd parked, along with some wolf paw prints. While it was interesting, she didn't give it much thought as her mind was still on the command. She slid onto the front seat and gripped the wheel, worried sick that something had happened to her parents or her sister. Why else would Naliana have summoned her? Not telling her folks she would be returning home before her studies were complete also concerned her, but they would be delighted by her unexpected arrival nonetheless.

Naliana was all about being mysterious. She loved to have fun with people, often at their expense. As much as Izzy had been looking forward to working with another Wendayan who had mastered the art of fire, her family came first—as did the command from above.

As Izzy headed out of the forest, more deep gouges ran alongside her old ones in the muddy road—gouges that hadn't been there before. A chill tripped up her spine, reminding her of the eerie sensation she'd had back at the water's edge of being watched and the paw prints by the car. She purposefully shook, trying to push that thought out of her head. If the humans found out about her powers and her kind, her life as she'd known it would never be the same.

RYERSON MCKINNON RESPONDED to the alarm by sliding down the fire pole. "Where's the blaze?" he asked one of his coworkers as he suited up. Shuffling feet and the distant sound of the truck engine firing up created a sense of chaotic excitement and intense urgency.

"Donaldson's warehouse. One truck's there, but they need more. Blaze is bad."

Shit. Abandoned for months, the building sat on the north side of the town of Silver Lake, but Rye hated to see anything in his area destroyed. He was the proud Alpha-in-training for his wolf-bear Clan that resided around the lake the town drew its name from.

Like his father, the instinct to protect and keep the Clan safe was strong and had him on high alert especially at a time like this when danger was close to their homes. He hoped the owner hadn't set the fire for the insurance money, as had been the case in a few other instances. Rye had heard Donaldson and his family had come upon hard times, so perhaps he'd been desperate.

"Let's hurry, folks," the driver shouted.

Rye hopped on the fire truck, wondering if the red moon was cursing Silver Lake once more. The townsfolk had their theories about why so much crime happened every time it appeared. He had his suspicions too, but he'd never voiced his opinion. The whole concept of evil werewolves would scare the town to death—or at least the human population living there.

They raced up Robin's Ridge and passed several cruisers along the way with their blue flashing lights illuminating the entire street. At the hardware store, Rye caught sight of a gaping hole in the front window and shattered glass on the sidewalk. What was wrong with people today destroying property? His best friend, Kalan Murdoch, one of the town's deputies, was probably running his ass off tonight trying to contain the crime spree.

A few miles before they reached their destination, Rye detected the acrid smell of smoke along with the glimmering light from the flames. For Donaldson's sake, he hoped they could save at least part of the building.

When they arrived, fire was rapidly consuming the left side of the one-story, vinyl-covered ten thousand square foot wooden structure, and it wouldn't be long before the other half was gone too. Fortunately, only a few buildings were located nearby, lessening the chance the fire could spread. Assuming it was arson, and Donaldson wasn't the one responsible for the blaze, why set this building on fire? No onlookers had arrived, and in his experience, arsonists liked to watch their handiwork. Without any bystanders hanging around to question, the *who* and *why* just got a bit harder.

Rye jumped off the truck and started toward the structure. Thanks to his enhanced werewolf hearing, a whimpering sound from inside reached him, but it was barely audible amongst the shouts of his coworkers, the crackling of the blaze, and the falling of a few roof beams. Shit. Fearing someone was trapped inside, he headed straight for his supervisor, adrenaline filling his veins. The men from the first truck who'd arrived were spraying the west side of the building, yet none of the men seemed to be on their way to search the interior, which meant he'd have to go into the undamaged end to find the source. "Sir, I think I hear someone crying in there."

Frank Emerson turned his head to the side and cupped his ear. "I don't hear anything other than the roar of the fire and the pump of the fire hoses."

Rye wasn't about to state the reason for his acute hearing since Frank, a human, didn't know his kind existed. "I have to go check, sir."

His superior grabbed his arm. "It's too dangerous. The building could collapse. You need to follow protocol."

If he did, the trapped animal or person would surely die. "I'll be quick, sir." Given his biological makeup, Rye was more immune to the heat and smoke than a human. He took off before his boss had the chance to stop him.

After calculating the speed with which the fire was consuming the west side of the building, he figured he had two, maybe three minutes tops to find the source of the crying. Rye prayed the trapped creature wasn't human. If he shifted, he'd be able to track the victim better, but shifting would have resulted in his suit being shredded, and he wasn't about to walk out of a burning building naked.

With no time to waste, Rye dashed into the far end of the building. If it weren't for his excellent eyesight, he would have had a hard time even seeing his hand in front of him. With the facemask on, he couldn't call out, so he slipped it off and nearly choked.

The deeper he moved into the building, the clearer the whimpers became, forcing Rye to press on despite the flames looming closer. "Can you hear me?" he called out.

A soft woof floated toward him and relief immediately washed over him. Hopefully, the little fellow was merely scared and not seriously injured. After calling out to the dog a few more times, a German Shepherd puppy hesitantly trotted toward him.

"Good boy," Rye said as he crouched down. "Come here."

A crack sounded and a beam crashed to the ground right next to him, nearly clipping his arm. The puppy whimpered and shook, and Rye closed the gap between him and his target. "We need to get out of here, little guy," he said, knowing full well the dog didn't understand him.

The puppy backed up, but Rye was able to scoop him into his arms before the dog darted away. With the animal held securely, Rye ran as quickly as he could toward the door. Just as he reached the outside, a ball of fire streaked next to him, causing a ton of wooden beams to crash down and even more smoke to surround him. *Boy, was that close.*

Needing to get them both to safety, he kept running until the air cleared.

Frank rushed up to him. "Damn, you were right. Are you okay?"

Ryerson took off his mask. "Yes, but I'm not sure about the pup here. He's still wheezing pretty badly."

"You shouldn't have gone in against orders, but we'll discuss it later." He nodded to the little fellow. "Isn't your sister a vet tech?"

"Yes."

"Then have the dog checked out now."

The puppy was still shaking in his arms. "Thank you, sir." He had another hour on his shift, but the dog might not last that long without care. From the back of the truck, he located a small oxygen mask and placed it over the pup's face, and immediately, the dog calmed.

Because he hadn't driven, he needed his sister to come and get them. He called Chelsea, and when she answered, he explained the situation and his location.

"I'll be right there. Keep doing what you're doing. He's probably still frightened."

"I hope that's all it is."

From the quiet background and lack of barking and cat howls, Chelsea must have already gone home, which was all the way across town. While Rye waited, he studied the fire. If Donaldson hadn't hired someone to torch the place, the Changelings were the next most likely suspects, though what they'd have to gain by burning the building, he didn't know. Then again, that group of malicious, mutated werewolves just might get a kick out of destroying something.

By the time Chelsea made it to the warehouse, the men had the fire pretty much under control, but the building was a total loss.

"Hello, there," Chelsea said, petting the rescued dog. She then looked up at Rye. "I don't see a collar on him."

"Looks like a stray. His coat is thin and he appears malnourished." Chelsea continued to rub the dog's fur and cooed at the poor animal while Rye held the mask over the dog's face. She acted as if time wasn't critical. "Shouldn't we be going?" Rye asked. "You can cuddle with him all you want after the vet checks him out."

After planting a kiss on the pup's head, she looked up at Rye. "I'm ready. What are you waiting for?"

"Funny girl." Still holding the puppy against his chest, he rolled his eyes, and then slid into the front seat of her car.

She inhaled deeply and wrinkled her nose as she fired up the engine. "Phew, you two stink."

"You would too, if you ran into a burning building."

She took off but not before looking over at the dog. "Was he burned?"

"I can't tell, but he didn't cry out when I checked him over."

"I called ahead and asked Dr. Dana to meet me at the clinic since we'd just closed."

"Smart." Once his sister and her new patient arrived at the clinic, he said he'd walk the two blocks back to the fire station to pick up his vehicle. He then handed her the puppy. "Thanks for coming out so fast."

"Anytime."

As soon as they were safely inside, he headed toward the station feeling a bit funny traipsing down the streets in his fireman's gear, especially on a warm summer night.

At home, Rye pushed open the front door and found his future Beta and second-in-command, Kalan, stretched out on the chaise lounge with a beer in his hand. The T-shirt Rye had worn yesterday was still on the chair next to Kalan, along with today's newspaper, but at least the coffee table was devoid of garbage like the pizza box from last night's dinner. "Not that I mind, but what are you doing here?"

"I needed a little energy release and wanted to see if you were up for a run."

"I'd like one, but I need to shower first."

Kalan waved his beer. "Do it later. By the time I finish throwing you in the dirt, you'll just have to get clean again."

Rye gave him the finger. "Don't you wish, but then you'll have to smell me."

"I'll suffer."

"Let me grab something to drink. My throat's dry." Rye walked past the four-seater dining room table into the open-concept kitchen and pulled out two beers since he noticed Kalan's was almost empty. He returned and handed Kalan his. "Here."

"Thanks. I heard about Donaldson's warehouse. Do you think it was arson?"

"Given the origin and speed with which the fire burned, it was definitely driven by an accelerant."

"Could the Changelings have masterminded it? It is a red moon tonight."

"Always a possibility. If they are responsible, they are probably just blowing off steam. Which reminds me, the fire truck I was on, drove by the break-in at the hardware store, and I saw the damage."

He nodded. "I worked that scene right after I checked out the graffiti sprayed on the back of the church."

"Sounds like kids might have been responsible for that."

Kalan polished off his first beer then opened the second. "That's what we thought, especially when we found the tipped over garbage cans behind the grocery store, but the break-in at the hardware store seemed a bit over the top for teens. Add in the fire, and I'm thinking those bastard Changelings are fucking with the town again."

"I wouldn't be surprised if they transformed themselves to look like local teenage boys then passed by a few security cameras just to throw us off." Rye slipped out of his hot uniform shirt, tossed it on the kitchen island, and then dragged his tired ass over to the sofa and sat across from his friend. "Why act up now when they've been rather calm for the last few cycles?" Rye asked.

"I wish I knew, but it's not like I can ask them or secure any kind of search warrant without probable cause. Nor can I go to the Sheriff and say there are some crazy ass werewolves causing trouble."

Rye chuckled. "That would cause a stir." The townsfolk of Silver Lake had no idea what kind of creatures lived in the hills north of town. Rye leaned forward and rested his elbows on his knees. "I've been thinking about the fire and why they might have targeted Donaldson's place."

Kalan's eyes widened. "Why is that?"

"Not that this is based on any fact, but the only reason would be to keep all of us so busy, we wouldn't catch them doing something else really bad."

"Such as?"

"The power hungry monsters might be looking for a way to steal more onyx. If they have us running around, putting out literal and figurative fires, they could search in peace." No one knew for sure why the Changelings needed the sardonyx so much, but it was suspected that it protected them from harm.

"It's as good a theory as any. What do you propose we do about it?"

Rye jumped up and paced. "Fuck if I know."

Kalan set his beer down then pulled his dirty blond hair back into a ponytail. "Perhaps a run will clear our heads. Unless you'd rather shower and head into town. We could find us some pretty little ladies and wear off our excess energy that way. You up for it? It might improve that sour mood of yours."

"Fuck you. I'm not *moody*. Irritated and a bit on edge, perhaps. As for going out, I don't have any excess energy. Hell, with all this shit that's been happening, I need to focus on taking care of our clan and not let some woman disrupt my brain."

Kalan laughed. "You better hope you don't meet someone claiming to be your mate."

"That would suck now, wouldn't it?" He didn't need any more talk of women. "Let's go for a run." Or rather a playful jaunt, as bears weren't built for speed. His wolf could run circles around Kalan.

Once they disrobed, they headed outside. The McKinnon compound consisted of six homes scattered across twenty acres with plenty of room around Silver Lake for additional buildings should the need arise. Kalan's family had an equal spread next to theirs. Since only shifters lived in this walled off region, they were free to run and roam without human notice.

Rye shifted into his wolf form first, and then Kalan became his bear. Good thing they were friends because Kalan could seriously harm him if he wished. It wouldn't take more than a few well-placed swipes to put Rye out of commission for a day or two. The same age, the two had chased, battled, and played together since their youth, helping Kalan learn his limits.

Despite having worked close to a thirty-six hour shift, Rye charged first, jumping on Kalan's back. The hulk swung around and knocked him off. Just to be a pain in the ass, Rye took off running toward his brother's house in an attempt to tire out Kalan.

"No fair. I'm too beat to chase you," he telepathed.

Rye was beat too. *"You said you wanted to go for a run. You change your mind?"*

"Yes."

It was only after their parents announced their retirement as Alpha and Beta that he and Kalan had been able to communicate telepathically, and the novelty had yet to wear off.

Rye loped back to his friend, and then went on the offensive, once more managing to get in a few good gouges before retreating. As they became more energized by having fun, their growls and snarls rang through the forest.

"Hey, you two," Chelsea shouted.

Rye stopped. Man, he hadn't even sensed his sister was near. He was losing it. Chelsea was carrying the puppy who appeared quite content. "I stopped by to tell you that Badger is going to be okay, thanks to you big brother."

Badger was a cute name, but in his shifted form, he couldn't tell her that. Times like this, the restriction of whom he could communicate with was frustrating and inconvenient. If he shifted back into his human form, however, he'd be naked. Usually that wasn't a big deal, but this was his sister, so he remained in his animal form. Kalan had enough sense to do the same.

"I don't want to interrupt your playtime, boys; I'm just delivering the good news." She held up a palm and continued, "No need to shift on my account."

Kalan roared.

"Because I don't need to see anyone's private parts, that's why, especially my brother's." She acted as if she understood what Kalan's roar meant. With a grin, she waved goodbye. "Later."

She spun around and rushed back the way she came. This time, Rye howled at her hasty retreat. As soon as she was out of sight, they shifted and headed inside to dress. As much as Rye enjoyed the quick tussle, his neck was stiff from Kalan flipping him over. He rubbed the sore area near his shoulder, hitting a sensitive spot.

"You should get a massage and have your aura cleansed at the Crystal Winds Spa," Kalan said.

"Great idea. While I'm there, I'll make sure to get a mani-pedi too." He glared at his friend. "Hell no, I'm not going to a spa. That's for women."

"Not true. Both our dads claim Kathryn Berta has the hands of a goddess. One hour under her talented fingers, along with some crystals and aroma therapy, and you'll be good as new." Kalan tapped his chest. "I've been, and afterward, I felt like a new man. In fact, after the day I've had, I might make an appointment for myself."

"You've never said anything before."

"Because I knew you'd ridicule me."

That was probably true, and if ever there was a time that he needed a clear head, this was it. "I'll think about it, but if I do go, you absolutely cannot tell anyone."

Kalan laughed. He made the motion of zipping up his mouth and throwing away the key. "Go take your shower, and I'll see you tomorrow."

As soon as his friend left, Rye hurried to wash off the stench and think. He loved his job and he loved his Clan, but he had a hard time prioritizing what needed to be his main focus. Should he work his way up the fireman's ladder so to speak, or throw all of his energy into being the best possible Alpha?

Right now, what he needed was a shower and a good night's sleep.

After the much-needed shower, Rye crawled into bed but found it was hard to turn off his brain, despite his exhaustion. He would doze for a while, and then wake up again thinking about the Changelings and what he and the other shifters could do to contain them.

By the time morning arrived, he was agitated and pissed off that he'd let himself lose sleep over those mutant werewolves. Even before he had a cup of coffee, he called the Berta home, hoping Kathryn could fit him in for a relaxing aura cleansing.

She answered after the first ring. "So nice to hear from you, Ryerson." He asked if she was free. "For you, I'll find the time. How about nine? We'll have your aura cleansed and your muscles relaxed in no time. In case you don't know, for privacy purposes, we do our cleansing for your family and the Murdochs at the house next to mine."

"Izzy's place?" he asked. Her parents had given it to her when she'd graduated from college, but she hadn't lived there in the last four years.

"Yes."

"Sounds great and thank you. I'll see you soon."

Once Rye disconnected, his energy actually perked up knowing he might soon be able to figure out a few things. He quickly brewed his coffee and fried three eggs and some bacon. By the time he had finished eating, he was running late and left his dishes in the sink.

He hopped into his black Ford Escape and headed down River-side Drive toward the Berta compound, admiring the sparkles shooting off the stream that connected Silver Lake to Wendayan Cove. He and his father had visited the Berta family last year when Kathryn's husband, Len, had needed some help.

A burst of energy speared him at seeing the well-kept, pretty, yellow house with white shutters. Sitting on about two acres, the wood frame home had a nice porch and a long pathway lined with flowers that led to the street. A small but well-tended garden was to the west of Izzy's single-story home.

Once he parked, Rye cut the engine and jumped out. Instantly, the sounds of the distant waterfall settled his nerves. As he continued up the pathway, he inhaled the sweet scent of the honeysuckle that bordered the path. Nice.

Rye knocked, and when the door opened, his body practically exploded with unbridled lust.

No, no, no. This couldn't be happening. Not now.

Chapter Two

RYE COULD ONLY stare. Izzy was more beautiful than he remembered. Her wide-set deep blue eyes shone with happiness and her full ruby lips were made for kissing.

"Rye! How nice to see you again." She held out her hand, not knowing that her presence was making his body go wild with need, his wolf demanding to be set free. "Come on in."

As soon as he shook her soft hand, his attraction magnified. With a five-year age difference, they had rarely run into each other during their school years, but even if they had, he had been nowhere near ready to be mated back then.

Was Izzy his mate? It sure as hell felt like it, but he wasn't happy about it or willing to admit it just yet.

The shifter community believed Naliana paired up people, and if that were true, he needed to find some way to make the goddess pay since this meeting couldn't have come at a worse time. As the future Alpha, if he ever did mate, it should be to another wolf.

When she stepped closer, her alluring scent invaded his body. Rye couldn't quite pinpoint the incredible aroma wafting off her, but it seemed to be a cross between some kind of day lily and hops. Whatever its name, her scent was addictive, provocative, and ever so captivating.

From her outward calmness, she didn't appear to have any idea they were destined to be together. "I hadn't heard you'd returned home," he said, not wanting to just stand there and stare.

A pretty pink hue tinged her pale skin. "My studies overseas were cut short. But enough about me. Mother said you wanted your aura cleansed." The soft, tempting way she said it sounded like water caressing a leaf after a long drought.

"Yes. With the crime spree last night, I need to clear my head." She smiled, and his damned dick turned harder than any crystal on one of the nearby shelves.

"Follow me."

The cozy living room was a combination of light blues, pinks, and greens. The large white sofa with its many tasseled pillows looked very comfortable, and he wondered if Izzy had picked out the furniture before she left the country or if her mom had come in and redecorated. An oil painting of the entire Berta family hung above the brick fireplace, but it was from her earlier years.

He wanted to ask why her mother wasn't here to perform the cleansing, but that would have been rude. Rye's dad had come here often to have his aura cleansed, and Rye now regretted not asking him what to expect during this cleansing process, but he'd been too damn arrogant to believe he'd ever need one.

Rye followed Izzy into a small room off the living room where a massage table sat squarely in the middle. The lights were low, soft music was playing, and the scent of incense filled the air. The crystals—pink quartz, black onyx, jade, and a brown stone he didn't recognize were displayed on a long, narrow table along the side wall. This, along with the lit incense, helped reduce the urge to do something about his mating call—at least for now.

Izzy nodded to the table. "Go ahead and get undressed, and then place the sheet over yourself. I'll wait outside while you get ready." She then quietly slipped out of the room.

Was she serious? He wasn't sure he could be naked anywhere near her and not embarrass himself. He rubbed the outline of his cock that was pressing hard against his jeans. This wasn't good. No way could he keep his erection from tenting the sheet. He'd have to roll onto his stomach and think of the Changelings, the horrid creatures they were. He'd do anything to take his mind off Izzy's tantalizing scent.

As he pictured the evil werewolves, his yearning decreased. He quickly undressed, and then climbed onto the table, pleased that he might survive this experience after all. Unfortunately, the moment she returned, his lust surged again. Her sweet fragrance once more invaded his body and wreaked havoc with his libido.

Once Izzy closed the door behind her, the room seemed to shrink in size. Pure disgust at his inability to control his desires slammed into him, and Rye inhaled to push out the prurient thoughts. Men for ages had been dealing with this whole mating thing, and none of them had died—other than from embarrassment—so he just needed to suck it up.

With his face planted firmly in the donut ring, he could only see her feet, but her soft footsteps were enough to indicate her every move. Two hard objects scraped against each other, and then her delicate scent drifted toward him again.

"Now relax," she crooned. "I'm going to pass these crystals over you. Let yourself feel the recharging aura soak deep into you."

He let out a breath, relieved she wouldn't be rubbing oil over his naked skin. If any part of her touched him, he'd be lost for sure. Damn Kalan for suggesting he come here. By the time Izzy was finished with him, he'd probably be more of an emotional mess than before he came, which defeated the original purpose of his visit.

Stop being a baby and let her do her thing.

Trying to take his own advice, he closed his eyes and attempted to push out his frustrations and angry thoughts. It was ridiculous that a woman he hadn't seen in years could affect him so much. He was built of stronger stuff. Rye would overcome!

For the next half hour, Izzy switched crystals, dragging them up and down his body while chanting words he didn't understand. Eventually, her soothing tone achieved the goal. His mind cleared somewhat, and his muscles finally relaxed.

She tapped his butt. "We're done. I'm going to step out now, but I want you to rest here for a few minutes. When you're ready, get dressed and come join me."

Not waiting for him to answer, she stepped out of the room. Rye was pleased she had acted totally professional but, dare he say, indifferent to him? Perhaps he'd made a mistake in thinking they were to become mates.

Embarrassed at not having asked enough questions about different species mating, he lifted the sheet and sat up. His intense sexual attraction was probably due to the fact he'd been under so much stress lately and hadn't bothered to find release with another woman in quite a while. This yearning and need must have been a result of his upcoming responsibilities within the Clan.

Confident he'd figured out the source of his recent discomfort, he slid off the table and tugged on his clothes, feeling stronger than ever. This aura cleansing sure had done the trick.

As he stepped from the room, Izzy was standing in front of the window, the light illuminating her sensually curvaceous body. Her auburn hair was tied back with a green velvet ribbon, and the sunlight streaming in the window created a halo around her. Any man would fantasize about her, so her being his mate wasn't creating this draw. Add in her other talents and she would be a fine catch— for another Wendayan.

She spun around. Her pupils had dilated as if she was now feeling something for him, but he dismissed it. The change from the bright sunshine to the subdued lighting of her living room must have caused it, or else he somehow reminded her of the bond between the Wendayans and the shifters. He thought he spotted some tiny sparks bursting off her skin but chalked that up to the backlighting too.

To test the theory that this attraction was merely lust and not because they were destined to be together, he thought it best to ask her out. His uncle owned a pub, and while it might not be the classiest place, it was safe and clean. "You interested in having a drink tonight at McKinnon's Pub and Pool?"

"A drink? Sure. I'd like that. It will be nice to visit with some old friends."

Good. Her apparent reason for going with him was as her escort. Her friends probably consisted of shifters as well as other Wendayans, so that made sense. His parents once mentioned that her mom, sister, and cousin interacted with humans on a daily basis, so Izzy's circle of friends might include them too. Regardless of the reason for accepting his invitation, Rye was happy to help. "How about I pick you up at seven? We'll eat some food and maybe shoot a game of pool."

She laughed. "I'm not sure I'll be able to control myself."

Certainly she didn't mean she wanted to ravish him. His ego wasn't that big. "Meaning what?"

She walked over to a table that had some loose paper on top. Holding her hand over the stack, she drew an imaginary circle above it, and suddenly the papers lifted and swirled. As she raised her arm higher, the papers floated upward. His awe increased proportionally with the height of the papers. She then lowered her arm, and as quickly as the papers flew, they dropped, a few missing the table on the way to the floor.

"That was incredible." He bent down to retrieve them at the same time she did and their fingers touched. Holy goddess. It was as if she'd plugged him in and then jacked up the electricity by two hundred or more volts. "Sorry," he said without thinking.

Rye swiped up both pieces of paper and stood. Izzy, whose top of her head only came to his nose, rose too, and his inner wolf wanted to devour her right there. He drew on his control and pretended as if his body wasn't about to transform in front of her.

She smiled. "I love testing my powers, but I fear I might forget where I am and move some balls."

His mind went into the gutter. "Balls?"

"Pool balls."

He swallowed a groan. "That's what I thought you meant. I agree that doing that at the bar would be difficult to explain." *Smooth, Ryerson...*

She reached out and grabbed his arm. "Don't worry. I promise to keep my magic restricted to the Cove."

"That's smart." Rye needed to get out of there. "I have to head back now. How much do I owe you?"

She waved a hand. "We never charge your family or the Murdochs. It's a courtesy."

To pull out a stack of bills would have insulted her. "Thank you. I'll pick you up here at seven."

"I'll be ready."

Not wanting to seem as if being in her presence made him uncomfortable, he walked instead of ran. The fresh air and scent of honey helped settle his screaming libido, but many more doses of Isadora Berta and Rye wasn't sure how he could keep from losing control and ravishing her.

ONCE RYE'S SUV disappeared from sight, Izzy needed something to keep her busy. She was out of sorts for some reason, something that never happened when she cleansed someone's aura. Trying to figure that out, she stepped into the massage room and straightened the already aligned crystals. Her stomach was twisting and churning at a hundred miles an hour. Sure, Ryerson McKinnon was divinely built with the most perfect ass she'd ever seen and shoulders wider than Silver Lake, but come on. Italy and France had their share of good-looking men too, but for some reason, none of them had made her want to do her magic for them.

There had to have been a reason why she'd shown off, only she didn't know what it was. There also had to be an explanation for why pricks of electricity were jumping up and down her body whenever she was near him.

Missy would be working at the spa in town, so there was no way Izzy would prance in and discuss her sexual longings with her sister when their mother was close by. Come to think of it, Mom had acted rather strange this morning when she suggested that Izzy take on Rye as a client. Hmm. Had Naliana given her mom a direct order? Even if Izzy asked her, Mom would never tell.

Perhaps it was time to get to the root of all this unease. Was it being around Rye or because Naliana had insisted she return home in the first place? None of her family members had been sick or in any kind of danger.

In the past, she hadn't been able to summon Naliana at will, but on a few occasions, the goddess had answered her plea. Had the white moon appeared instead of the red moon yesterday, Naliana would have descended from the heavens to enjoy her conjugal visits with her immortal husband right here in Silver Lake.

To improve Izzy's chances of making a connection, she picked up the pink quartz, held it to her chest, and then closed her eyes. "*Naliana, may I speak with you?*"

No matter the number of times the goddess had contacted her, Izzy was always a bit nervous. When the goddess didn't answer, Izzy thought Naliana might be upset that she'd played with the papers in front of Rye, but it wasn't as if the shifters weren't aware that the Wendayans had talents beyond normal humans.

"*Naliana?*" She tried to telepath her goddess again.

After patiently waiting a full minute, Izzy set down the crystal and hopped up on the table, needing time to think.

Elana. While her best friend from high school was human, the two of them had shared everything—including the knowledge that werewolves existed. Her friend had always been her sounding board when the kids bullied Izzy, and she in turn, had listened to Elana when her home life turned particularly bad. In fact, for much of middle school, Izzy spent more time with Elana than she did her own sister. It wasn't surprising since Izzy and Elana were in the same class in school and her friend practically lived with them.

Now more than ever, Izzy needed a level head. She called her friend who answered immediately. "Blooms of Hope, Elana speaking."

Pride swelled. Izzy had helped Elana name her flower shop. The

Hope part came from the fact Silver Lake was in Hope County. "Hey, it's me. Do you have a minute?" She'd seen Elana yesterday but only briefly.

"Sure. I'm just cutting the tips off some flowers and making sure the arrangements I've made still look fresh. What's up?"

"It would take too long to tell you now. Are you up for an early lunch?"

"Sure, where?"

"Nate's Pizzeria in about twenty minutes?"

"Perfect. See you there."

A bit giddy at being able to have a girl chat like back in school, Izzy changed into a pair of capris and a cute pink tank top and headed out. Because she had a few minutes to spare, she decided to see what new herbs Natalie Fremont, another Wendayan, had at her herb store. As soon as she walked in, however, Izzy realized stopping there had been a mistake. A slew of enticing fragrances sprang out at her, and she wanted to sniff each and every one of them. She instantly recognized she would need hours instead of mere minutes.

One side of the shop was lined with dried flowers and plants. While Izzy had the ability to find herbs and flowers that could ease her worries, she wasn't good at locating any that would help settle her stomach. That ability belonged to her sister, Missy.

With Natalie's help, Izzy bought the appropriate herbs then headed over to the pizza shop. When she entered, Elana was waiting for her by the entrance. The two of them were such a contrast—Izzy with her unruly auburn hair to Elana's dark brown, thick locks. Izzy was five-foot eight, whereas Elana claimed to be five-foot two, though that was probably only when she wore heels.

"Hey there," Elana gave her a hug. "So tell me what's so important that you'd skip out on work."

Since they arrived before the lunch rush, Nate's was mostly empty but would probably be packed around 12:30—or at least it used to be that way four years ago. The sign at the front said to *Seat Yourself*, so they snagged a booth in the back. While the décor was a little tacky, the red and white-checkered tablecloths and lit electric candles reminded her of some of the restaurants in Italy.

"Mom said she didn't need me this afternoon. Besides, I worked this morning." The waiter came over, and as soon as they ordered drinks, Izzy leaned forward. "What do you know about Ryerson McKinnon?"

Elana's brows rose. "From the gleam in your eye perhaps I need to ask what you know about him. You've been home all of two days, and he already seems to have you hot and bothered."

Perhaps coming here had been a bad idea. Elana may not be able to relate to what Izzy was going through. A human without powers might not understand what it was like to be drawn to a shifter in such a strong way. "Let me start from the beginning, so you'll understand what's been happening. About a week before I came home, I sensed a presence."

"You mean like a ghost?"

"No. This presence was creepier than a ghost. It was a man who was quite talented at following me without me catching onto him."

She sucked in an audible breath, her eyes wide. "You have a stalker?"

"Had a stalker. Yes. I'd been in Scotland for only about two weeks, when I sensed someone following me, only I never actually saw him." She held up her hand. "And don't say it was my imagination. I can sense things, you know."

"I believe you. I'm just glad you listened to your sixth sense. Is that why you came home months sooner than you'd planned?"

Elana was the only person outside of her family who Izzy had kept apprised of her schedule. "Yes."

That was a white lie, but it couldn't be helped. While she was convinced Elana would never give away Naliana's secrets, Izzy thought it better not to tell her friend about the gods in heaven and their abilities. Some things would be too much to handle for the human mind.

"Are you still scared this guy will come after you?"

Izzy smiled. "No. Not all the way from Scotland. And I didn't say I was scared, but I wanted to be cautious." She held up a hand. "I wouldn't have said anything, but I brought it up because I didn't want to keep anything from you."

Elana leaned back against the padded seat and let out an audible breath. "Thank you."

"The reason I called you was because this morning my mother gave me some lame excuse about why she couldn't do Rye's aura cleansing, and then said to be sure to give him a long, hard massage."

Elana placed a hand on her chest then looked around, probably to check if anyone was listening. She leaned forward again. "You saw him *naked*? Was he perfect? Not that I've noticed, but he and his friend Kalan, are both so hot."

Relief washed through her. If Elana swooned over the idea of being next to a naked Rye, then it made sense she might be affected too. Sure, Izzy had special talents, but deep inside, she was still a female. Any woman would have swooned over the tribal tattoo integrated with a wolf paw around his upper arm. "I couldn't touch him."

Elana's brows pinched. "Why not?"

"Without thinking, I asked him to take off his clothes and slide under the sheet. Only then did I worry that if I saw the outline of his cock, I'd want to jump his bones. Touching him might have caused that to happen."

"You should have jumped his bones. You told me you didn't do anything with anyone while you were in Europe."

"No one really excited me. Besides, you know what would happen if a human found out about my powers."

Elana nodded. "He'd feel inferior and not be able to get it up. But Rye's a shifter, right? That means he has powers, so you're equal."

"Our powers are different, but yes we both have abilities."

"Did Rye question why you didn't give him a massage?"

"No. I had wondered why he didn't say anything, but since this was his first cleansing, he might not have known what to expect."

Elana nodded. "True. I heard his dad is stepping down as Alpha, and Rye will be taking over as soon as his father returns from his vacation."

She was happy for Rye, but that didn't change things between them. "The problem is that I haven't been on a date in so long, I'm afraid I'm going to mess it up."

"Going to?" Her eyes widened. "As in, he asked you out on a date?"

A giggle escaped. "Yes, tonight."

Elana lightly clapped. "Where to?"

"McKinnon's Pub and Pool."

The server came over, and once he took their order, he headed back to the kitchen. Elana unfolded her napkin and placed it on her lap. "I still don't know what the problem is. Are you afraid you'll end up sleeping with him?"

Heat raced up her face. "Shh. I don't know."

"Isadora Berta. I've never seen you this flustered."

She wished she knew the cause. "I know, right? Rye is just a man." One with thick, dark hair she wanted to run her fingers through, and eyes so green she'd do anything to be able to dive into them.

"To say he's *just* a man is a stretch."

"Fine, he's just a man like I'm just a woman."

"I'll ask you again. What's the problem? You're both consenting adults."

She was twenty-seven, old enough to have the urge to settle down. "He's five years older, a hot fireman, and about to be the Alpha of his Clan, which means he's busy. Not only that, I don't want to do anything stupid. What if I become too excited and let loose a power or something?"

Elana giggled. "You mean if you inadvertently light a fire under his ass?"

She'd mentioned what she'd been able to achieve in Scotland.

Thankfully, werewolves healed quickly if she did let a fireball escape. "Yes. I've just returned from being away for four years, and I have no business even thinking about getting into a relationship. I should settle in first."

"Did you take a class in excuses over in Europe, because that's all I'm hearing? When you go out with him tonight, have a good time. It's not as if you have to marry the dude. Sheesh. News flash— women are allowed to have fun before they tie the knot."

Heat raced up her face. "You're right. I don't know why I'm so worried. I'm going to be in a public place with lots of people. Nothing is going to happen."

Elana leaned on her elbows, her brows raised. "There's always afterward. You live in your own little cottage and he lives in a place by himself too. I say, let whatever happens, happen. There's nothing wrong with having heart pounding, to die for sex. And after you two decide to have the fun escapade, I want every detail."

Oh, boy. Izzy was in for a tongue-lashing tomorrow regardless of the outcome.

Chapter Three

RYE TOSSED THE old newspaper in the trash then picked up his scattered clothes from the living room. As he dropped them into the laundry basket, his mind raced. He could use someone to talk some sense into him, but Kalan wouldn't be off work for another hour, and he needed to leave soon for his date. Even if his folks weren't on a cruise, he probably would have been too embarrassed to speak with his dad about what it was like to be with a mate. It wasn't just the sexual attraction that made him think Izzy was the one, though it had been his first clue. Hell, any man would want to make love with her, but there was something else going on. He'd be damned if he understood it though. Being around her twisted his stomach into knots, and her scent drove him wild and made his inner wolf howl.

For the last few hours, he'd been debating the issue of her being his mate. He'd gone back and forth so many times that he might as well have plucked the petals of a daisy in a love-me, love-me-not fashion.

Rye stepped into the bathroom one more time to make sure he looked okay. He ran his fingers through his slightly shaggy hair. He'd need to have it cut soon, especially with the Alpha ceremony approaching, but waiting another week wouldn't hurt. He could shave again, but many women said they liked the scruffy beard look.

Good to go.

The faded jeans and plain white button-down shirt was a little dressed up for the Pub, but Izzy deserved better than some ratty, slogan T-shirt he usually wore when he shot pool.

His goal for tonight was all about assessing the situation. If Izzy wasn't interested in going out again, he'd pull back. In a week or so, he'd conveniently run into her and perhaps ask her out again. He wanted to understand what excited her, and then plan from there.

Time to go.

The drive along the river had to be one of the prettiest in Tennessee. When the leaves changed in the fall, he loved to head into the Appalachian Mountains to run or ride his bike, confirming he didn't want to live anywhere else but in Silver Lake.

At two minutes past seven, Rye pulled into her driveway. Perfect. He didn't want her to think he was anxious, yet he wasn't the type to keep a woman waiting. Whatever happened tonight, he had to keep his cock in his pants. That much was a given. Rushing her might ruin the chance of her wanting to see him again.

As he walked up the pathway and spotted the flowerbeds, it was clear a classy, world-traveling woman like Izzy was probably used to having a man bring her a gift when they went out. Shit. He hadn't even thought about that. The men from Europe were probably experts on how to treat a lady too. He hadn't been on a real date in so long that he'd forgotten what it was like to be with someone sophisticated.

Well, hell. If there was any chance she wanted to be with him for any length of time, she'd have to take him exactly as is—someone who kicked his feet up on the coffee table, drank bear out of a bottle, and left his crap all over the place. If she couldn't handle that, then it wasn't meant to be.

He rang the bell, shuffling his feet for a few seconds before forcing himself to still. A future Alpha had no reason to be nervous. He had a good job, money in the bank, and was about to be in a role of authority.

When Izzy opened the door, all those thoughts evaporated, and every cell in his body exploded. He immediately tossed out all the reasons why she wasn't his mate. She was his. She had to be. He couldn't help but stare at her black silky top that hugged every curve. Wow. Hot and sexy didn't come close to describing her. While her beige shorts were of modest length, the platform shoes made her legs look a mile long. If she'd pulled her hair back instead of letting it hang loose, he might have been able to keep his eyes in their sockets. And her lily scent woke up his wolf. He hoped to hell she didn't glance down and see the bulge in his pants. Goddess in heaven. This might have been a mistake. How had he forgotten what being around her did to him?

Rye instantly glanced behind her in the hopes he could keep his body from transforming in front of her.

"You want to come in?" she asked.

It would have been polite to say yes, but if he did, no telling what he might say or do. "Could I take a rain check? I forgot to eat lunch so I'm rather hungry." That was a blatant lie, but nothing else came to mind.

Her mouth parted in sympathy, and the urge to kiss those luscious lips nearly tossed him over the edge. Rye glanced down for a moment, disgusted at his lack of control.

"Let me get my purse then."

Izzy appeared so cool and calm. Hell, even if she were his mate, he didn't deserve her. A moment later, she came out then locked up. He thought it strange she'd take such precaution since he'd never heard of any crime in the Wendayan Cove area before, but he didn't want to embarrass her by asking. Perhaps after living in Europe, she'd learned to be wary.

Without thinking, he placed a hand on her back as he led her down the pathway, and sizzling sparks shot straight through him. Fuck. "Are you happy to be home?" he asked, needing something to take his mind off his traitorous body.

"I am. I missed my family so very much."

He opened the passenger side door for her and watched her slide in, her long legs stirring the wolf in him once more. Rye jogged over to the other side and hopped in. "I heard you planned on staying longer."

Kalan had found out from Mrs. Berta that Izzy wasn't to return for another month or so, which meant there had to be a reason why her studies were cut short.

Firing up the SUV, he backed out of her driveway then headed into town. Rye glanced over at her, but she was staring out the window. "What is it? You can tell me." He thought about the flying papers this morning. "Did someone get hurt when you used your powers? Is that why you rushed home?"

"No! It's nothing like that."

He waited for her to elaborate, but her lips remained in a thin line. Clearly, this was a sore subject. Just as he was about to drill her again, she twisted in her seat toward him. "Naliana summoned me home."

His grip firmed on the wheel, and his pulse soared. "You spoke to the moon goddess?"

Had it been the white moon, he would have understood. His father had taken him to visit Naliana and her husband, James, a few times, but she had never communicated with him or his father when she wasn't on earth.

"Yes, but our conversation was short. She asked I go home, and when I asked her why, she told me to just obey."

"That sounds like something she'd say. When you returned, did you find out what was wrong?" Both the bears and wolves looked out for the Wendayans.

"No, and that's what puzzles me."

Rye tried to think back about Naliana's other requests while she was in her human form, but he couldn't remember her asking any member of his Clan to do anything like that. "How did she sound?"

"What do you mean?"

"Was her tone urgent? Or did she seem upset with something?" Rye made a left onto High Point Street.

What sounded like a snort came out. "I didn't think about it. I was in shock when she spoke."

"I would have been, too. What were you doing at the time?"

She stilled for a moment and then said, "Oh, my."

"What?"

"It hadn't occurred to me there might be a connection between my unease during my last few days in Scotland and Naliana's contacting me."

Rye didn't like the way this sounded. He pulled into the parking lot of his uncle's bar, cut the engine, and then faced her. "Back up a minute. Tell me what made you worry." His tone might have come out too demanding, but his protective nature had kicked into high gear.

She ran a hand down her top and his thoughts short-circuited for a moment. When his nails extended due to his lurid thoughts, he dug them into his pants leg to distract himself, but it didn't work as well as he would have hoped.

"I went to Europe to learn from other Wendayans who are well-versed in manipulating air, wind, fire, and earth."

He whistled. "I saw what you did with those papers. Are you saying you can do other things too?" He'd been aware that her cousin Teagan had premonitions, and her sister could help heal injuries, but he wasn't aware of any Wendayan who possessed multiple talents.

Her face turned pink. "Yes, but it's not something I brag about."

Now he felt bad and cupped her hand. "I didn't mean to pry. Are you hungry?" He would finish the conversation inside.

She smiled. "I know you are."

Rye slid out of his seat and rushed to the other side. This time when he placed a hand on her shoulder to help her out, his libido didn't explode though it did flare. Perhaps his concern for her had interrupted the mating call for a moment.

He led her inside and the aroma of beer and peanuts assaulted him. Rye should have given more thought as to whether this was a good place to bring a woman like Izzy.

Separated into two rooms, the poolroom was in the back and

contained five tables. The large, noisy front area had a long, polished wooden bar against the east wall, a stage on the north side with a small dance floor in front, and booths along the other two walls with some scattered tables on the south side.

"It's a bit loud," he said. "If you want to go to the Lake Steakhouse, we can head on over there."

Her eyes sparkled. "What? Are you afraid you might lose at pool?"

He remembered her comment about being able to move the balls around. "I won't unless you cheat."

She grinned, looking like a mischievous imp. "I promise to behave."

He waved to his little brother, Finn, who was managing the bar. "Let's sit at a booth in the back," Rye said.

Wanting as quiet a spot as possible, he led her to the south side, away from the noise. His cousin Molly rushed over. Oh, boy. Every one of his brothers would hear about his date in a matter of minutes.

"Hey, Rye." Molly glanced over at Izzy. "Welcome back. Long time no see." She gave her a hug.

"Four years to be exact."

"Wow, it didn't seem that long."

As nice as it was for the girls to catch up, this was his date. "I'd like a Heineken." He looked over at Izzy. "What would you like?"

"A Cabernet."

Molly winked, understanding the hint that he wanted to be left alone. "You got it."

As soon as his cousin disappeared, and before other well-wishers arrived, Rye wanted to finish their conversation. "I want to get back to what happened overseas."

"You aren't going to let that topic drop, are you?"

"Not a chance."

She waved a hand. "Okay, it was probably my imagination, but I thought someone was following me."

He didn't like that one bit. "Animal, mineral, or vegetable?" He didn't want her to think he wasn't capable of some levity.

That brought a smile to her lips. "I don't know, but from his ability to disappear at will, I'm thinking it could be *your* kind."

"You make that sound bad."

"Not all are good."

His first thought was a Changeling. "What made you suspicious?"

She lifted one shoulder. "Just a feeling. I wish I were like Teagan, as she would have known what it was. I can't sense one, but right before *you-know-who* contacted me, I was at an inlet practicing my skills when I felt the hairs on my neck rise—literally. I turned around and spotted a gray wolf with a distinctive white patch on his forehead just standing there."

His gut churned. "What did he do?"

"He ran away. At first, I wasn't sure what to think, but when I reached my car, I noticed fresh tire tracks next to a set of paw prints."

"That's what made you think he might be like me. If he shifted into his wolf form, he might have returned to his car then shifted back into his human form, which would explain the paw prints."

"That was what I was thinking. I should have looked at the spot where he'd been hiding. I might have seen some discarded clothes, but I just wanted to get out of there. Before I even reached my car, I was contacted by *her*." Izzy glanced upward.

"Her timing could have been coincidental or she might have been watching out for you." The members of his Clan believed Naliana was aware of everything that went on in their lives. "Regardless of the reason, I'm glad you're back in the States."

"Me too," she said with a smile that seemed more than just someone who was happy to be home.

Molly returned with their drinks. "You know what you want?" She glanced between them.

"Give us a minute, please," Rye said.

"Sure."

Izzy picked up her menu. "Will you get ribbed for being out

with me?"

That came out of left field. "Why should I be?"

"I don't know. Maybe because I'm not your kind."

He appreciated she was trying to be discreet in public by not saying the word *werewolf.* An Alpha having a non-werewolf mate might never have happened in the past, but if they were destined to be together, he didn't mind being the first. "I honestly don't care what people say since it's none of their business." Though as late as yesterday, he was in denial about the possibility.

"I agree."

When Izzy folded her menu, he raised his hand for Molly. She came over, and they both ordered. "So what do you like to do for fun?" he asked, wanting to learn more about her.

"Fun? Practice my skills." Her brows rose, clearly trying not to say anything that would tip off the rest of the human population about her extensive abilities.

"Anything else? Do you like to ride horses, bowl, watch movies, work out, or what?"

"Are you interviewing me for a job?"

Oh, shit. He hadn't meant it to come off like that. "No. I guess I'm out of practice being around a beautiful woman." *And one whose fragrance is driving me crazy.*

The tension in her shoulders seemed to disappear. "Thank you, but I didn't peg you as the shy kind."

"It happens now and again." *When I'm with someone who means a lot to me.* It seemed as if someone had lined his boots with lead. He was sinking faster and faster with each word—proof that he cared too much.

This is Izzy. Enjoy.

She leaned back in her seat. "Since you asked what I like to do for fun, I'll give you the quick lowdown about me. Growing up, I always had the sense my parents expected great things from me. Taking time to run around with the regular kids was hard, because I was too excited to see what new things I could conquer."

"You turned out okay."

"Thank you, but I never really fit in. Being me could be daunting at times. I'd see someone struggling and want to help, but to do so would expose my powers."

He'd never thought about how hard it would be to stand by helpless. At least if a fight broke out, he could lend a hand as a human. "That would be tough. I'd live in guilt."

"I do sometimes." She cleared her throat as if she didn't want to speak about herself any more. "What about you?"

Compared to Izzy, his life was mundane. "I grew up like everyone else, except that I had a few extra talents."

She smiled. "Like the ones that came in handy on the football field?"

He gave her an evil eye. "I'll have you know that I pumped iron more than anyone on the team, though I won't deny being a natural beast didn't hurt."

She chuckled, just as he'd intended. "I was only kidding, you know."

Rye enjoyed teasing her back. "Uh huh."

"In all seriousness," she said, "Despite your normal upbringing, you did very well for yourself. Not many thirty-two year olds are asked to lead a large group of men and women."

"I wish I could say I've earned the honor, but those things are handed down from one generation to the next."

She shook her head. "Don't be so hard on yourself. Your father wouldn't have stepped down unless he was confident you were ready."

He'd like to think so. "Maybe, but time will tell."

His cousin waltzed up with the food and placed the first plate on the table. "Chicken for the lady and a hamburger for Rye. Bon appetite." She grinned, spun around, and rushed off.

"Molly's looking good," Izzy said.

Rye wasn't sure how to respond. Telling Izzy she looked better probably wouldn't be welcome. "I think it's because she's happy. She likes working here, at least for now."

They both dug into their meals. Halfway through, the front door opened and Rye glanced up, his senses reacting to the presence of a *Were*. Four people came in, but none were shifters he recognized, and he didn't like it one bit.

"What is it?" Izzy asked, concern lacing her tone.

Chapter Four

RYE LOOKED IZZY straight in the eye. "Nothing. I thought a friend had come in, but I was mistaken." He smiled then dug into his meal with gusto, proving his earlier claim that he had been hungry.

She wasn't sure she believed him. Twisting around to check it out, two of the men who entered were carrying some electronic equipment they then brought up on stage. "Are those the Lakewood Boys?" Izzy hadn't seen them since high school.

Rye glanced up. "Sure are. They're good too."

"I remember enjoying them." She hoped it wouldn't become so loud that they couldn't talk. Having been on her guard for the last four years, it was so nice to be able to relax and not have to worry if she slipped up.

Rye seemed intent on eating quickly, but she couldn't tell if it was because he didn't know what to say or if he couldn't wait to show off his pool skills. She'd played the game perhaps three times in her life and was terrible, but hopefully, she could convince him to give her some pointers.

Normally, she wouldn't have bothered asking him, as she doubted she would play again, but something about Rye made her want to be near him. And that voice! Holy crap, it was so deep and sexy, she could listen to him talk for hours. The only real issue was that he kept sending out mixed signals. At times, he exuded such control, especially when his protective side flared up, but every time she tossed him a smile, he looked away—and that confused her. He had seemed interested in her talent and not at all afraid of what she could do, yet something about her seemed to shove him off balance.

Regardless of how he acted around her, for the first time in her life Izzy was actually interested in him—as a man. She always figured she would end up with a Wendayan for obvious reasons, but she saw no reason not to branch out. It didn't hurt that she loved the way he smelled, and just watching him move made her wonder what he would be like in bed. As for playing pool, if he were willing to help, having the hunky man draped over her wouldn't be a hardship.

Wanting to get on with their date, she set down her utensils, and finished off her glass of liquid courage.

Rye looked up. "You finished?"

"Yes, but don't let me stop you."

He pushed his plate away. "Don't want any more. You want to play some pool or would you rather go out for a walk? I'm good either way."

No he wasn't. He seemed to love pool and wanted to play, but she appreciated how concerned he was that she have a good time. One of the Lakewood Boys tapped the microphone, did a quick sound check, and then strummed his guitar. "Pool's good, but go easy on me. I'm a newbie."

He gave her a cheeky grin then slid out of the booth. "I have a feeling I'm going to get my ass handed to me."

"Trust me, that won't happen." Not unless she redirected the air from the vent, which she'd never do in public.

With his hand on her back again, he led her past the bar into the back room, and that one gesture made her feel warm, safe, and rather turned on. What was it about Rye that had her pulse soaring? Perhaps it had been too long since she'd been with a man. When she was near him, all her feminine parts tingled, and she suspected she glowed a bit too, but hopefully nothing that was noticeable.

Two of the five tables were empty, and he walked up to the one near the far wall. "First we need to find you a cue stick," he said.

She didn't think it mattered which one she used, but apparently, he wanted her to have the best experience. Rye had her test out a couple, and because she was tall, she decided she preferred a longer stick. Izzy inwardly giggle. What woman didn't like a big one? "This one's good."

While he arranged the balls, she watched some of the other players. Their power and accuracy impressed her. If only they'd been Wendayans, they might have been able to channel their talents into something quite helpful.

"I'll break," Rye said. "Unless you want the honors?"

She'd much rather watch his tight ass bend over the table than make a fool of herself anytime. "Have at it." After taking aim, Rye pulled back the cue and then jammed it forward, his muscles flexing. The cue ball hit the stack and sent them scrambling. "Wow."

He smiled then immediately refocused. This was a different side of the man—driven to succeed—and she liked that.

"Looks like I have stripes, so you get solids," he said.

Because a few of his balls had fallen into the pockets, Rye took the next shot. After chalking his cue, he lined up his stick. *Smack. Pop. Drop.* Izzy clapped. "Nice job."

"Thank you." He studied his shots. With a light tap, the white ball hit a striped one, but the ball clipped the corner and bounced off. "Your turn."

Izzy wasn't normally giddy, but the challenge excited her. Perhaps there was more to pool than she had thought. "Hmm. Which one should I try for?"

"I thought you didn't want to cheat."

She opened her mouth. "It's not cheating if I request some help."

He grinned, acting as if he'd been waiting for her to ask. "Okay, then. Let's try to sink the number three ball into this side pocket."

She knew the fundamentals of angle of incident equaling angle of reflection—or something along that line—but that didn't mean she could put the ball where she aimed. After walking around the table, she leaned over to take her shot.

"Wait," Rye said. He came up behind her and slid his hands down to her wrists, his face inches from hers. His groin was snug against her ass, and it was clear she wasn't the only one turned on.

She was tempted to turn her head and kiss him just to see his reaction, but of course, she wouldn't. What she really wanted to do was grind herself against him and then have everyone in the bar disappear so they could make love on the pool table.

Stop fantasizing. She couldn't help it since him being so close messed with her entire electrical makeup. Izzy stood still, took a deep breath, and rotated her fingers on top of the cue stick. "Like this?"

He adjusted her hands. "More like this. Now choke up on the stick then aim right here, but don't hit it too hard. You don't want to sink the cue ball."

Choke up. Aim here. Don't hit it hard. Sheesh. He'd be better off teaching her how to ride a motorcycle or something. "Okay. I got this." Rye stepped back, but his presence was affecting her ability to concentrate. Trying to do as he instructed, she slid the stick back, and the end of the stick rammed into him.

"Whoa," Rye said, as he whipped the cue stick right out of her hands.

She spun around, her gaze going straight between his legs. "Where did I hit you?"

"In the worst place possible."

Oh, no. Heat raced up her face. The devil in her wanted to ask if she could rub it and make it better, but she didn't want to scare the poor man away. "Sorry. Maybe you should stand on the other side."

"Good idea." He croaked out a response, but when he grinned, she figured he hadn't been hit that hard. Rye handed her back the cue then moved across from her. "Give it your best shot."

Wanting to make him proud after that fiasco, she closed her eyes to imagine the trajectory then struck the ball. *Click, clack, thunk.*

"You did it!" Rye sounded truly happy for her. He trotted back her side of the table and slapped her palm in victory.

As much as she enjoyed the little celebration, what she really wanted to do was throw herself in his arms. After the ice between them was broken, they just had fun. Rye was great about helping her, but in the end, he sunk the black ball to end the game.

The music was going full blast, and while she enjoyed the tunes, a lot of people had come in and the place was becoming rather stuffy.

"You want to head back?" he asked, undoing the top button of his shirt.

"Sure. The noise is making it hard to talk."

They put their cue sticks up, found Molly, and asked for the bill. "I'll pay at the bar," he told his cousin.

"Works for me. Just leave a big tip."

Rye laughed. "Don't I always?"

"I guess." His cousin grinned. "I'll see you around, Izzy."

"For sure." It was good to be back among old friends. Izzy had been only a year ahead of Molly in school, but they'd enjoyed many of the same activities during that time.

Rye waved down his brother Finn and paid his tab. "Let's get out of here."

Because a group was on the dance floor, Rye placed his hands on her waist and guided her outside. Once in the fresh air, she inhaled the sweet scent. "It was a bit stuffy in there."

"It was."

After he made sure she was safely strapped in his SUV, he took off toward Wendaya Cove. She tried to imagine what the next few minutes might bring—and what she wanted them to be like. Izzy was tempted to ask him inside for a drink, but if he turned her down, she'd be upset. It wouldn't matter if he claimed he had Clan business to take care of. It would be best to let him take the lead. After all, he had asked her out.

The drive home seemed to take only seconds. Rye pulled into her driveway, and after he cut the engine, hope surged. He slipped out of the vehicle, and then came around and opened her door. While she was capable of opening it herself, she was a bit old fashioned and appreciated the chivalry.

"Thanks for dinner and pool," she said. "I never realized how much fun it could be."

He smiled. "We'll have to do it again."

Yes! "I'd like that."

By the time they reached the front door, her pulse was pounding. She was twenty-seven and anything but a virgin, yet here she was as nervous as a teenager on her first date.

He moved in close, and when he lifted her chin, her heart nearly jumped out of her chest. "I want to see more of you, Izzy."

Her knees almost gave way. If she thought he wouldn't freak, she'd take her top off right there to show him more. "I'd like to see more of you too." *Especially after what I felt pressed against me at the bar.*

He leaned over, wrapped an arm around her waist, and kissed her, instantly melting her heart. His lips were soft and full, and the contact had just the right amount of pressure. As if her arms had a will of their own, she wrapped them around his neck. Wanting, or rather needing more, she opened her mouth to invite him in. Rye groaned and swept his tongue inside, tasting like hops and smelling like the outdoors. Pulses of erotic need raced up her arms. If her eyes hadn't been closed, she would have noticed the blue glow. As she leaned into him, Rye broke the kiss.

"If I don't stop," he said, "I might have to invite myself in, and I think you've had enough of me for one night."

No, she hadn't, but his sincerity thrilled her. "Again, thank you."

"Make certain to stay safe. Always be aware of your surroundings."

What was that supposed to mean? Izzy could have told him that no one could harm her as her powers were, well, powerful, but she figured it was best to keep quiet. No need to let her protector know that she could probably take care of him.

Taking a few steps backward, he kept his gaze on her until he spun around then dashed to his car. His reactions always seemed so inconsistent, but perhaps that was what made him so interesting. When she told Missy and Teagan about her date, perhaps they could help her decipher the Ryerson McKinnon puzzle.

AS MUCH AS Rye had wanted to ravish Izzy, what he'd said to her was the truth. That kiss had set his body on fire, and if he hadn't stopped, no telling what he might have done. He'd spotted her blue essence, convinced she wanted him also, but it was too soon. It was better to give her time to think things through. Rushing her could end in disaster.

Just short of gunning the engine, he pulled onto the road and headed east toward the lake, his mind reliving every delicious touch and smell of Isadora Berta. She was perfect. While she was a great sport at pool, especially since she tried so hard at improving her game, her aim sucked. He could see many lessons in her future.

Rye was halfway to the compound when his headlights shone on a car stranded in the road. The sedan had its emergency lights flashing, and while he didn't recognize the silver Toyota, he slowed, hoping he could be of some help.

Pulling off to the side, he put his SUV in park and slipped out. As he approached the vehicle, he sensed a shifter and looked around for the owner. Despite his excellent eyesight at night and heightened sense of smell, he didn't see him or her.

"Hello?" Rye called, but he received no answer. Hoping the person hadn't passed out in the car, he edged his way toward the vehicle.

He was so focused on trying to find the driver that the crunching of a stone right behind him took a second to sink in. Rye was only able to turn partially around when sharp nails dug deep into his back, sending streaks of pain to his brain. What the hell? Rye twisted to return the attack, but a knife to his gut ended his ability to fight effectively. As much as he wanted to shift, his body gave way, and he dropped to his knees.

The masked attacker darted over to his car, and as he pulled open the door, he turned to face him. "That was your one and only warning."

Rye's vision swam and he concentrated on shifting, but he was too weak. Gravel flew through the air, followed by the stench of burnt rubber. Motherfucker.

Get help.

Rye couldn't tell if he'd thought that to himself or if someone had spoken to him, but it sounded like good advice. His first thought was to head back to Izzy's, but his house was closer—assuming he could keep from passing out while driving.

Kalan would be working, and unless Connor, his brother, was out on a surveillance job, he should be home. Using every ounce of effort, Rye called him.

"What's up? I thought you said you were taking Izzy out tonight."

Izzy. Yes, he should still be with her, but he wasn't.

"Rye?"

"Someone stabbed me." He barely choked out the words.

"What? Where are you?"

Rye's mind muddled. He really needed to shift. It was the only way not to bleed out, but he couldn't focus enough to do so. Connor had asked him something. Oh, yeah. Where was he? Damned if he could remember the name of the road. "Just left Izzy's…"

"Hang on, I'll be right there."

Before he could tell his brother he could make it home on his own, Connor disconnected. What had he been thinking? Rye didn't need anyone to rescue him. He was the Clan's future Alpha. He tried to stand, but his head swam and he lowered himself back to his knees. Fuck. Humiliation shot some adrenaline through his system, and he managed to crawl on all fours to his Ford. Being this low to the ground as a wolf didn't bother him, but the position as a human sucked. With dogged determination, Rye reached his car. Drawing on all his strength, he dragged himself onto the driver's seat.

Finding his keys took some doing, as did getting the stupid key in the ignition, but he was finally able to start the car. When Connor didn't find him on the road, he would head on over to Rye's house. It couldn't be more than two miles. He could make it that far.

The first mile Rye drove slowly, working hard not to pass out. His shirt and pants leg were soaked with blood from the stab wound. The gashes on his back didn't appear to be critical, unless they became infected. As hard as he tried to hold onto the wheel, his vision kept blurring.

"Naliana, I could use a bit of help here."

Rye didn't really expect her to answer. She wasn't known for being a Good Samaritan in the truest sense, but it was worth a try.

His eyes suddenly rolled back in his head, and he jerked to stay alert, but the front tires had a mind of their own. The car rolled off the pavement and onto the berm. As if some invisible force grabbed the wheel right out of his hands, the vehicle careened to the right. He blinked, barely registering that he was heading toward a tree. A second later, the airbag exploded into his face and the vehicle slammed into a hard object before coming to a stop.

Chapter Five

"**R**YE, CAN YOU hear me?" came a voice from above. Rye must have passed out. Someone was calling to him, but he couldn't quite identify the familiar sounding voice as severe pain stabbed through his gut. It felt like someone was pressing on his mid-section, making it hard to breathe.

"You need to shift, buddy."

Buddy? That had to be Connor. His brother was the only one who called him that. Why did he need to shift? One more push and the rush of blood finally reached his brain, enough for him to open his eyes.

"That's it. Shift. Izzy's in trouble," his brother said.

Izzy was in trouble? His protective instinct immediately took over, blocking out all other thoughts and propelling him into fight mode. As his bones cracked and his fur flew, his vision turned white hot from pain. Someone must have set him on fire because everything hurt. Once in his wolf form, he tried to go to her, but Connor held him down.

Rye growled and bared his teeth.

"Stop moving. You're injured. Izzy's not in trouble. I lied to get you to shift. That stab wound is deep and the gashes on your back are almost as bad. Lie still and let me wrap your gut."

While Rye understood each of the words, they weren't making any sense as he could only focus on the fact that Izzy wasn't in trouble. The words *stab wound* jarred his memory. He'd been taken by surprise. Damn. Because it took too much energy to stay awake, he closed his eyes and let Connor do his thing. Somehow, his brother had managed to get him home.

A hand shook him. "Rye, wake up."

He wanted to stay asleep, but he cracked open an eye once more. Connor was standing over him again. "Missy's here to do some healing with you."

He was about to ask why when a wave of pain washed over him, but this time it wasn't as bad. Only then did he realize he was in his wolf form, and Missy was staring at him. Well, shit. He wanted to ask her not to mention this to her sister, as Izzy would think he wasn't worth much if he couldn't even sense someone sneaking up behind and clawing him, but he wasn't about to shift back into his human form just to ask her. Wendayan or not, she was a human and would probably freak if she saw a naked man that she didn't know very well.

Missy moved toward him with a burlap bag in her hand that smelled of cinnamon, cloves, and some other spices he couldn't identify.

"I'm going to put this under your head," she said. "It should help with the pain."

While his head pounded from a migraine, it was his back that stung and his gut that was cramping. Given that he had very little strength, he was willing to try anything that might help.

Missy placed the soft sack under his neck, and then walked back to the table. With interest, he watched her light candles and then place what looked like leaves in a glass. What that would do he had no idea, but soon she began her chant and waved several crystals around. Within minutes, the ache in his stomach eased. Hmm. Perhaps there was more to this Wendayan stuff than he'd always believed.

After another fifteen minutes of doing spells, candle lighting, and crystal waving, Missy packed up, leaving the candles glowing. "Rye needs to rest," she told Connor. "By tomorrow, he should be feeling like his old self."

That was great news. Connor walked her out and then returned a minute later. "Since you aren't going to die on me, I'm going to head on home, buddy. You rest until tomorrow, but call if you need me." He blew out the candles and disappeared.

Rye actually obeyed and remained in his shifted form. Since the pain was lessening with each minute, he fell into a sound sleep and woke the next morning feeling refreshed. After shifting back into his human form, he headed toward his bedroom. As he passed his phone sitting on the table, he swiped it and saw a message from Kalan stating he'd be over a little after noon. To his surprise, it was already close to that now. Since Rye had slept so much, his wounds must have been rather serious.

In the bathroom mirror, Rye checked out his injuries. The scratches, or rather gouges, on his back seemed to have healed quite well, and even the wound on his stomach had completely closed up, though it was a bit tender. He couldn't imagine how humans survived without being able to shift in order to rejuvenate. He never would have needed Missy's help in the first place if he hadn't lost so much blood from the sneak attack. Somehow, his healing genes hadn't kicked in until after Connor was able to convince him to shift.

Needing to clean up, Rye hopped in the shower and watched the caked blood rinse down the drain. He lifted his arms to test if there had been any permanent damage, and found he had full range of motion with no pain. After further inspection, he deemed himself healed.

Starving, he washed quickly, dried off, and then dressed. As he finished fixing a ham and cheese sandwich, someone knocked on the door then pushed it open. After closing the door behind him, Kalan entered the kitchen area. "Hey, you're alive."

"Am now."

"Last time I saw you, you were in pretty bad shape."

"When were you here?" He didn't remember the visit.

"Connor called me as soon as he brought you home, and I came over. I stayed about an hour but then had to go back to work."

"I appreciate you stopping by."

Kalan sat at the counter and grabbed half the sandwich Rye had just made. "Watch it," Rye said, though he wasn't angry.

"Now that you appear to be coherent, tell me exactly what you remember. Connor told me something, but I want to hear it from you."

Rye explained how he was coming from Izzy's when he stopped to help what he thought was a stranded motorist. "It was a set-up, though how my assailant knew I'd be coming down Riverside Drive is anyone's guess." He explained that he'd left McKinnon's around nine and driven Izzy straight home.

"He could have followed you from the bar."

Rye stilled, remembering the sensation of knowing a werewolf was near, but not being able to identify him. Now he wished he'd paid better attention. "It's possible."

"Connor said you mumbled something about it being a silver Toyota."

"Yes."

"I checked with both rental companies and neither has any record of renting a Toyota that color, so I pulled a list from the DMV." He shoved the paper toward him. "I highlighted those owners who are werewolves. Then I followed up to see where they might have been last night."

His friend worked fast. "And?"

"All have alibis."

Rye studied the list of three. "Tim Smithfield has to be seventy and I don't see the other two fitting the size. This means the guy rented the car elsewhere."

"I agree. Can you describe him?"

"He was shorter than me by a couple of inches, though by the time I turned around I was a bit hunched over from the knife in my gut." The average man was only five ten, making his assailant all too common.

"You sensed him though, right? I don't remember anyone ever getting a drop on you."

"I was thinking of Izzy and locating the stranded motorist and wasn't paying attention until I heard him behind me, but he was definitely a shifter." This was further proof Izzy was his mate. He'd been all consumed thinking about her and had pushed aside his other instincts.

"What did he smell like?"

Rye had to think. "Wool and the slightest hint of perfume or some kind of exotic cologne."

"Could the cologne have come from hugging a woman?"

"Maybe." Rye snapped his fingers. "He told me that this was my one and only warning."

Kalan pulled out his iPad and jotted down the information. "What do you think he meant by that?"

"I've been wracking my brain, but I can't figure it out. I don't think I've pissed anyone off lately."

"Could he have mistaken you for someone else?" Kalan asked.

"It's possible. My back was to him." Rye snapped his fingers. "He had a different accent. It sounded either British, Irish, or Scottish. I could have been mistaken as I was in a lot of pain."

"You're saying he was a foreigner?"

"Yes." He remembered that Izzy believed someone in Scotland had been following her, but he couldn't be positive the two were related.

"We don't get too many folks from across the pond here in Silver Lake. If he's still around, he'll find it hard to hide in this town. I'll put out some feelers."

"Thanks."

Kalan moved over to the fridge and pulled out a beer. "Have you told Izzy about the incident?"

"No."

"Why not? You afraid she'll think less of you because you let someone get a jump on you?" Kalan razzed him.

Rye held up his middle finger. "I've been ill."

"Better call her soon. She must be wondering what happened to you."

"I figured Missy told her." That was lame. "I'll call or stop over tomorrow." *Just tell him.*

"Tell me what?"

Oh, shit. Had he just transmitted that thought? "Izzy is my mate."

"Well, hot damn!"

TODAY WAS IZZY'S day off from working at the spa, and she was anxious to tend to her garden. During the last four years while she was studying in Europe, her mom had taken care of the flowers, herbs, and vegetables, and Izzy hoped she could keep it looking as nice. Sure, she could hover her hand over the plant and make it grow tall and strong, but doing so wouldn't provide her with a sense of accomplishment. No, she wanted to see if she could grow vegetables and flowers the old-fashioned way.

With trowel in hand, she knelt down in the dirt and dug a hole, needing to plant a small rose cutting her mother had given her yesterday. Once it was deep enough, she gently placed the roots in the ground, and then firmly packed the dirt around the stem.

She sighed. Izzy should be excited to be home doing the things she loved, but she was still so unsettled. Rye hadn't called her yesterday, and here she thought their date had been a ton of fun. The kiss afterward had been amazing and so full of promise, and from the way he kept studying her and smiling, she was sure he'd felt the same intense attraction. Guess she'd misunderstood his cues. It was no surprise. She hadn't kept up on the dating protocol in the States, so maybe he expected her to call him. Hopefully, Elana and Missy could provide some answers.

"Well, well. Hello, Isadora," said a voice behind her.

That tone and that accent had her memory whirring as she tried to recall if she knew him. No one ever called her by her formal name.

Twisting around, she stood then wiped her hands on her pants. People didn't wander onto Wendayan land, and this man acted as if he was some long lost relative. He wasn't much taller than she was, and from his pasty white skin and red hair, he didn't get out much. "May I help you?"

"I hope so, as I've traveled a long distance to meet you."

A shiver started at the base of her neck and worked its way down to her toes. The increase in her pulse turned her mouth dry. "What do you mean?"

He forced a smile, but there was no joy in his eyes. "I saw you perform an amazin' feat in Scotland and wanted to find out more about your talents."

Her heart nearly stopped. "You must be mistaken." The odious man moved closer and Izzy held her palm over the newly planted rosebush. "You aren't supposed to be here. Please leave."

"I came for something, and I won't leave without it." His forceful words had her blood pressure shooting skyward.

Izzy drew herself up to her full height of five foot eight and stared him in the eyes. "If you've seen my talents, then you don't want to make me mad."

"What are you plannin' to do? Shoot a fireball at me? You'd have a lot of explainin' to do, lass, if you killed me."

If he'd seen her do that, he might have been the werewolf. *Think, think.* Rye would know what to do, but he wasn't here. Summoning her powers, she lifted her hand, drawing the thorny rosebush upward. His eyes widened as if he understood what was about to happen, but didn't really believe it. With a flick of her wrist, the plant shot forward and wrapped around him.

"What the fuck?" he shouted. The man struggled and tore at the vine that kept weaving its way around his body.

Try to get out of that mess, Mr. Scotsman. Not wanting to listen to his shouts or screams, Izzy rushed back inside the house. Taking only a second to grab her keys and purse, she locked up, and then jumped in her car. All she could think of was running to Rye where she'd be safe.

Chapter Six

AFTER A FULL day to think about what he was going to say to Izzy, it was time for Rye to set things straight with her. Coming right out and stating they had something special happening between them might unnerve her, but telling her she was his mate would definitely be over the top. They'd only been out on one date.

Even though he knew they were destined for one another, it didn't mean they would become mated unless Izzy accepted him. For that to happen, it would take work on his part.

Most likely Missy had told Izzy about the incident, and Rye was a bit surprised she hadn't called yet to ask about him, but perhaps he'd misread her interest.

As he was about to find a shirt to put on, there was a knock on his door, and his body immediately reacted with waves of lust.

Izzy was here.

He had no idea, if she'd be concerned or angry that he hadn't called. As he pulled open the door to say hello, the words left him as he steeled himself against the intense body-assaulting waves of desire.

Dressed in tattered jeans and a body hugging green T-shirt, she looked amazing, despite her pinched mouth and the lines around her eyes. Her hands were smudged with dirt, and both knees were stained brown. This wasn't a social call.

"May I come in?" she asked. A hint of fear emanated from deep within her, and his wolf tried to claw his way out. He tamped down his overwhelming urge to hold and protect her.

"Sure."

Izzy glanced back over her shoulder as if she believed someone had followed her, and then ducked inside. That one action had his gut twisting in knots. He had so many questions, but he didn't want to scare her by going all Alpha and protective mate on her and ask what was going on. Because of his worry, her intoxicating scent thankfully wasn't eliciting the usual reaction.

"How about we sit in the living room?" he asked. Izzy stepped farther inside his house and glanced around. He'd never taken much time to decorate. The black leather sofa set and large screen TV screamed bachelor pad and surely wouldn't appeal to the lovely woman before him. "Can I get you something to drink?"

"No. I'm fine."

She sat on the sofa, and he took the seat facing her. Perhaps it was for the best, as being near her interrupted his thinking.

She glanced off to the side as if something was weighing on her mind. "I think my stalker followed me here."

His heart lurched so hard, his incisors sprouted, and his bones cracked. Her hand clasped her chest, and she sucked in a deep breath. Hating that he startled her, Rye drew in his inner wolf and forced his heartbeat to slow. The changes disappeared, and he was once more fully human. "Sorry, I didn't mean to lose control like that."

"It's all right. You just took me by surprise. It's not like I haven't seen a shifter before."

That might be true, but most likely not very often. "Tell me everything," he demanded. "And leave nothing out. I want to know even the smallest detail about this stalker."

ONCE IZZY SAW the scars on his body, she hadn't wanted to burden him with her own problems, but her comment had just slipped out. She nodded. "Do you remember I mentioned that someone, probably a werewolf, might have been watching me the day I was practicing my magic in Scotland?"

He sat up straighter. "Yes. Don't tell me you think he's here?"

"I know he is. He showed up while I was in the garden and said he followed me. He also said he came for something, but he didn't say what it was."

Rye scrubbed a hand down his chiseled jaw. "What does your stalker look like?"

She thought it was an odd question, but she answered anyway. "He's an ordinary looking man. He has few muscles, red hair, and white skin. Oh, and a long, thin nose. He's at my place now if you want to see him for yourself."

Rye jumped up. "What? What do you mean he's at your place?"

"Don't worry, I twisted a vine around his body then came straight here."

"That was smart." He paced in front of her. "He's still at your house?"

"He should be, unless he was able to get loose. The vine loses its power after a while, and if he shifted into his wolf form, he'd be able to get away. It wasn't like I had a lot of time to think about my plan."

His lips firmed, acting as if she'd done something wrong. "Fuck." He looked at her. "Sorry." While she was pleased he was taking her seriously, something else was going on that she needed to find out about.

Her gaze dropped to his gut then back again. "Rye, tell me what's wrong."

He placed a hand over his reddened skin. "It's a long story. If you're wondering why I didn't call yesterday, it was because I ran into someone after I left your house." He tapped his stomach. "Hence the wound."

She sucked in a breath. "You wrecked your car? Is that why I didn't see it in the driveway?"

"Yes, but that was afterward. Let me start from the beginning." He continued to pace while he explained about the stranded motorist and then about the clawing and the stabbing. "I'd like to say I was some kind of hero in all this, but I believe in total honesty." Rye then told her how he'd had to crawl on his hands and knees to reach his car, and instead of waiting for Connor to help him, he'd been so damned stubborn that he passed out behind the wheel and crashed.

"That's terrible. Did you recognize your attacker?"

"No, but the man who attacked me had a Scottish accent. That's why I asked you what he looked like."

Her heart pounded. "Do you think it's the same person?"

"It sure seems like it. I want to find him and make sure he never comes near you again."

She clenched her fists. "The man only threatened me, but he never touched me. It's not like you can ask the police to arrest him for talking trash."

His brows furrowed. "He might have harmed you if you hadn't stopped him, but you're right. We can't go to the police and tell them how you controlled him."

"I know." If the humans learned of her powers, there was no telling what might happen. Exposure was one of Izzy's biggest fears. The rest of her family also had some abilities, but nothing as obvious as creating cyclones or parting the sea, though her dad could set a forest on fire. "If you didn't get a good look at him, how can you be certain if he's the same person?"

"From his reaction at seeing me alive. His voice will also let me know. Then I'll teach him a lesson about messing with you." The vehemence of his statement took her aback. Rye acted as if he really cared.

He threaded both hands through his dark, thick hair, and she lowered her gaze to his muscular pecs and flat abs, which distracted her to the max. "Let me take a look at your injuries."

She stood, stepped over to him, and then turned him around. She lightly dragged her fingers down his back. "This looks painful."

"I don't need you to feel sorry for me. I'm fine. Really."

She didn't believe him and stepped around to face him again.

She ran a finger over the scar on his stomach, and heat from his skin caused a trail of hot desire to shoot up her spine. "This doesn't look fine," she said.

"It barely hurts. The red will be gone by tomorrow."

She wasn't as convinced. This close, Izzy studied the tattoo that banded his bicep. "What does this stand for? I get the wolf paw, but why a lightning bolt?"

He inhaled deeply as if to keep his voice even. "The bolt cutting through the tribal symbol stands for power, and the wolf's paw is rather self-explanatory. It's the same one on my back. My dad has had the face of the wolf on his arm since he became the Alpha."

"What about the wolf claw on your shoulder?"

"The McKinnon's have had both for generations. To be honest, I've never questioned it." He held up his palms as if he'd had enough of her scrutiny for now. "Let me throw on a shirt and then we can go."

He disappeared down the hall. It wasn't just his protective nature that appealed to her, it was also that he treated her with respect. The fact that her body went into overdrive every time she was near him was an added bonus.

WHILE SHE WAITED, Izzy took a moment to look around. Rye's house could use a woman's touch that was for sure. The white walls and monochromatic furniture screamed practical and masculine. A few well-placed crystals here and there would do wonders for his health and liven up the space. As she dragged her gaze toward the kitchen, she halted. Before she could figure out why Missy's crystals were here, Rye walked in all dressed in a tight black T-shirt totally distracting her.

Once she regained her equilibrium, she nodded to the candles. "Those look familiar."

"They should," he said matter-of-factly. "Connor asked Missy to come here and help with my healing. I needed the extra boost from her powers in my weakened state even though I was in wolf form. I have to say, she worked magic—literally."

His rapid healing pleased her, but she was a bit miffed that Missy hadn't told her about Rye's injury. She and her sister would have a little chat later. "She never said anything about your injury or that she helped with your healing."

"She's a professional."

He did have a point. Izzy and Rye left to check out her place. As she stepped outside, she took in her surroundings first before continuing on to her car. If this stalker could follow her from Scotland to Tennessee without her knowledge, he was one slippery bastard.

"Mind if I drive?" Rye asked.

Izzy swiveled around to face him. "I thought you said you wrecked your car."

"I did." He held out his hand, apparently for her keys.

"I'm a good driver."

"I'm sure you are, but if I sense the shifter is near, I can react faster."

That made sense, but the real reason was probably closer to the fact he needed to be in charge. There wasn't time for a debate, however. "Here you go."

"Thank you."

For most of the short drive to her house, Rye said little. It was as if he was concocting a game plan in his mind.

"When we get there," he finally said, "I want you to stay in the car and lock the doors."

Now he'd gone too far. "I should be telling you that. If I had wanted to kill the man, I could have already. I just didn't feel like answering questions about how I ended up with a body burned to a crisp in my back yard."

A small smile lifted his lips. He then glanced over at her. "I think I should see a demonstration of what you can do."

Her powers had grown to such a scale that she hadn't even told her parents the extent of her abilities. Besides, her magic was highly personal, and she wasn't willing to share it with anyone yet, let alone a man who she didn't know all that well.

But you want to know him better said that little voice in her head. *Maybe...*

The problem was that while Rye appeared to be interested in her, like so many others before, he would eventually feel threatened by her powers and leave.

As Rye neared her house, her stomach churned. She really didn't want to see the man again, yet she didn't want him gone either.

"Is the garden in the back?" Rye asked.

"Yes," she said as she pushed open her door and started to get out.

"Izzy, please?"

"Fine." She didn't want to see the jerk anyway.

Rye slid out his side of the car. "Lock the doors. If you see him, drive away."

She'd never leave Rye to fend for himself, but she decided to keep quiet about that. "Ask him what he wants from me."

"Oh, you can bet I will."

He jogged toward the back of her house and then disappeared from sight. Her chest cramped in anticipation of what he might find. She appreciated that Rye wanted to protect her, but there was no need. She could handle whatever came her way.

Tapping her foot, she looked around, making sure that the nasty man wasn't lurking somewhere, just waiting for her to return.

A few minutes later, Rye came back, his gaze continually searching the area. He climbed back in her car. "He's gone, and there's no sign of him anywhere."

She leaned her head back. "Really? Did you peek inside the house and check behind the trees?" She held up a hand. "Never mind. You didn't have to. You could sense he wasn't there."

"That's right."

"Do you think he'll go after my family?"

"I don't know, but I don't want to take any chances." The tension had returned to his voice many times over. "And you have no any idea what he was after?"

"He just said that he came for something and wasn't leaving without it. Since he stalked me in Scotland, he can't want something I keep in my house." She huffed out a breath. "I need to warn my family."

"Well, shit."

Chapter Seven

OWEN CHANCELLOR WAS pissed. No. He was more than pissed. He was Changeling mad at himself and at Isadora. She was supposed to become his wife and do what he wished. How dare she ensnare him in a vine—with thorns no less. He was so furious that if he weren't in his car, he would find the biggest tree and smash his fist through it. With his shifter strength, he could leave a hell of a hole, which would help release this built up anger and frustration. He didn't like being on edge one bit.

Isadora would not get away with treating him that way. The only reason he wouldn't take out his anger on her right away was because he hadn't even explained that he wanted to take her back to Scotland to become his wife.

One thing was for sure though—she needed to learn to obey. He would show her he was the one in charge, and it would be a lesson she soon wouldn't forget. He just needed time and a bit of witchcraft to help him.

It had been easy to locate *his* own kind in the hills of Hope County, and he had to admit that these American Changelings were nothing like that man with Isadora. Rye was his name—or at least that was what he thought Isadora had called him when he was showing her how to play pool.

It had taken Owen a few well-placed bills to find someone who could direct him to their black witch. Seems the Changelings in this part of the world had to hide just like they did in Scotland.

Glancing down at his phone, he checked the GPS again. This witch lived high in the hills, far from Silver Lake proper—if one could call a town with a population of less than ten thousand proper at all.

When Owen pulled into the driveway, an old woman was standing on the lawn in front of a house that looked as decrepit as the old lady herself. The wooden structure was worn and tired and didn't appear to ever have been painted. While all of the windows had glass in them, two didn't have shutters. With a few missing boards, the front wrap-around porch wasn't in any better shape.

That creep he'd paid to give him this woman's name must have told her to expect him, though he couldn't even guess how she could know what time he would be arriving.

Then again, she was a witch.

Owen slipped out of the vehicle, and after he approached her, the old woman folded her arms. "You wish a spell?"

Good, he wouldn't need to explain much. "Yes. I need a strong one to bind a woman's powers."

Her brows pinched. "How powerful is she?"

Giving too much away might send other American Changelings to find Isadora, and he couldn't afford to lose that gem. "She can make plants grow with a twist of a hand."

The woman's eyes widened. "Powerful indeed. You have the money?"

"Yes, half now and half later." The weasel he'd found was a good haggler for the old lady. Most likely, she'd give him a cut of her exorbitant fee.

Owen didn't care about the cost though. He'd come this far for Isadora, and he wouldn't leave without her. Timing was key. Isadora would be on her guard for the next few days, so he'd wait as long as was needed. He wanted her unsuspecting when he took her.

"Come inside," the black witch said.

He'd always held a healthy respect for witches, especially one who was a Changeling, so he did as she asked. The inside wasn't in much better shape than the outside, however, the worn but serviceable furniture looked clean.

She waddled over to a table on the east wall and picked up a simple burlap doll along with a ball of sisal. The doll's eyes were made from buttons and the mouth from yarn. She returned to him. "Do you have something of this woman's?"

"Yes." From his pocket he slipped the green velvet ribbon that had fallen out of Isadora's hair when she ran back to her house after imprisoning him. He held it out.

"Good. Attach the ribbon to the doll then carefully wrap this twine around the body. Start by threading the string through her legs then around an arm, across her neck or head, and finally back to the other side. When you are done, every inch of the doll needs to be covered. Then the arms must be secured against the body. That is the only way her powers will be bound."

Excitement raced through him. "Anything else?"

"Yes." From her pocket she extracted a piece of paper. "Hold the doll high in the air and say this spell. The deed will then be done."

He read over the words, pleased the instructions were simple. In the past, he might have dismissed this voodoo stuff as nonsense, but not anymore. Not since a witch had placed a spell on his sister.

Owen extracted an envelope from his pocket and handed it to the witch. "When I find she is no longer able to use her spells, I will return with the other half."

She cocked a brow. "Don't even think about cheating me."

"I won't." It might be the first and only time he'd actually follow through with a promise.

RYE WAS CONCERNED. A man had come over from Scotland because Izzy had something he wanted. The tangled vine in her garden had been torn into pieces, but the lack of even a scrap of cloth implied her stalker hadn't shifted. "I want to come with you when you speak with your parents," he told her.

A flash of something he couldn't identify crossed her face. "I can do it alone."

He started her car, happy she let him drive. "It's not a question of being capable. I'm sure your dad will be highly upset this has happened. I'm hoping between us, we can come up with a plan. I have resources. Not only will my Pack help in any way, the bear Clan will offer their services too. Together, we can take him down."

Her smile wobbled, but it appeared sincere. "Thank you. It's still a little early. Dad will be at the cell phone store until eight, and Mom is probably at the spa."

He glanced at the clock on the dash. "How about we grab a bite to eat then head on over?"

"That sounds wonderful."

While not all wolves were good, those who were Changelings were always bad. Because his uncle's pub wasn't as nice of a place as Izzy deserved, he took her to the Lake Steakhouse. He didn't have reservations, but hopefully it wouldn't be too busy on a Thursday night. Besides, the hostess was a member of his Pack.

Rye was able to find a parking spot near the restaurant, and once inside, Katie, the hostess smiled at them. "Nice to see you again, Rye. It's been a long time."

He didn't need to have a discussion on his habits with her. "It has been. Table for two, please?"

Katie picked up two menus and asked them to follow her. Once seated, Izzy glanced around and then leaned forward. "Do you think my *admirer* could be like those who live in the mountains?"

He appreciated her subtlety. "It was my first guess."

"I probably should know this, but how did they end up so evil? My dad told me and Missy some crazy tale about mutated animals, but I didn't understand it."

Rye was surprised she didn't know the history, especially since she and Naliana seemed to be on such close terms. "Naliana's husband was the one who shared the story with me. How much of it is true, I don't know, but it seems plausible."

"Dad told us that long ago a group of wolves became rabid and that the townsfolk wanted to put them all down."

He nodded. "That was what James told us. The infected wolves were all corralled, ready to be killed the next day. Rumor has it, the night before the slaughter, two pregnant females and a few unaffected males escaped with the help of the others. Apparently, those two women didn't exhibit any signs of having rabies, but their babies' genes mutated nonetheless. That allowed those werewolves to change not only into their wolf form, but also into anyone else they met. One touch and they could walk away and change into that person— but only when the red moon is in the sky, and only up to three days afterward." He shrugged. "I'd say it's an old wives' tale, but I swear bad shit always happens on that night."

Izzy's mouth opened. "That's horrible."

"Agreed." Rye had seen proof of these Changelings taking the form of someone else, but he didn't need to be discussing that topic in a restaurant.

"Because this man had touched me, he might have been able to change into someone who looked like me?" she asked.

Rye didn't like how her voice had escalated. "Yes, but he wouldn't have any of your powers."

"Thank goodness for that."

"Over the years, the Changelings have bred with other wolves, but their evil genes were passed on." Rye had evidence regarding a lot of other issues with the Changelings, but it would be better not to frighten her further.

The server stopped by to take their drink order. Izzy had asked for a red wine at the Pub. "We'll split a bottle of Cabernet Sauvignon." He glanced over at her. "Does that work for you?"

"Perfect." From her tone, she seemed a bit impressed that he even knew what wine to order.

"Do you know what you want to eat?" he asked. As much as he'd like to spend hours with her at dinner, they still needed to meet with her parents.

Izzy looked up at the server. "What do you suggest?"

"Do you like beef, chicken, or fish?"

"All of them."

Rye chuckled. "How about we order two filets?" She nodded. "How do you like it cooked?"

"Medium rare," she said.

"Make that two."

The server left, and Rye leaned back, wondering how someone as amazing as Izzy Berta had ended up his mate. The timing sucked for starting a relationship, but the more time he spent with her, the more he wanted to thank Naliana—assuming she had sent Izzy home to him.

Izzy picked up her napkin and placed it on her lap. "Do you think that man will come back even though he knows what I can do to him?"

Lying would serve no purpose. If he told her no to placate her, she might let down her guard. "He seems very determined."

"If I thought it was something I owned, I'd invite him into my home and tell him to take what he wants and then leave."

Rye reached out and clasped her hand. "He's dangerous, and you can't forget that."

"I can stop him."

It didn't matter if she could or couldn't. "If you harmed him, the world would learn of your powers." Tension rippled across her features. Not that he wanted to expose the ugly reality, but Rye believed it was necessary. "The scrutiny would not only change your life and your family's lives, but many others in town."

She blew out a breath. "I know, which was why I didn't inciner-ate him."

"I don't think you're capable of harming anyone like that, especially when you weren't positive what he was after."

"True."

Thankfully, Izzy seemed to understand. "All I'm saying is please be careful."

She stilled. "You said that to me after we kissed. Did you suspect something then?"

"No, I just didn't want anything to happen to you."

She smiled and Rye's insides twisted. He wasn't sure how much longer he could last without making love with her. The problem was that she had no idea what she meant to him, and for the time being, it was for the best.

"Thank you, but you don't need to worry about me. I'll keep my life a secret."

It was in his genes to worry about her. "Good. Now that you're home, what do you plan to do? Keep working at the spa?"

"I'm not sure. Mom has Missy and Teagan working there now, so I don't know if there is enough for me to do. I did earn a degree in chemistry, so I might apply for a teaching job."

Izzy didn't seem like the type of woman who was willing to be a burden on anyone. "I think you'd make a wonderful teacher as long as you weren't tempted to do some tricks for them."

She grinned. "I know, right? If an experiment I set up didn't work, I'd want to use my magic, but I wouldn't."

He chuckled. "You said Naliana told you to come home. Do you think it had anything to do with your *friend* who came to visit?"

"I've given that a lot of thought."

"Have any theories yet?" His pulse sped up thinking that perhaps Naliana had sent her home to him.

"While the people in the Cove understandably don't go around showing off their skills, I believe mine are now the most powerful and versatile."

"If you can control all those forces, you might be."

The lines around her eyes tightened. "That leads me to believe I've been brought back to be our protector."

That had merit. "I see myself as having the same role, only with my group." Rye wanted to say that despite her extensive talent, if she wasn't careful, bad things could happen. He'd say nothing tonight since she had enough on her mind. "Who do you think you need to protect the Wendayans from?"

"Maybe these Changelings," she whispered. "Especially if they are anything like my Scottish stalker."

"Once more, I'll caution you. You've been gone for quite a while. When the next red moon appears, see what happens, but don't ask too many questions, or they could target you."

She visibly shivered. "Way to make me feel safe."

He reached across the table and clasped her hand in his. "I wouldn't have said anything, but you seem determined to help."

Her shoulders relaxed. "I've seen you for all of two days, yet you seem to understand me quite well."

Rye wasn't about to tell her about the connection already forming between them. Just then their food arrived and they dug in. Her small moans of pleasure drove him crazy, and his cock was so hard he was ready to take her on top of the table. Using all of his restraint, he resisted.

"This is so good," she said. "Great suggestion."

"I'm glad you like it." The food was excellent. He probably should eat here more often, but dining alone wasn't his thing. Readying to take over the leadership from his dad had kept him too busy to even find a woman to date. In the back of his mind, he wondered if he had been waiting for his mate all this time.

As they sipped their wine and ate, warmth suffused his body. Being with Izzy was good for his soul. She listened to what he had to say and seemed to take his opinions seriously. She was not only beautiful but poised and caring.

After they had both finished their meal, he motioned for the check. When the server delivered it, Izzy placed a hand on his.

"It's my treat."

"That's not the way I fly. I asked you, so I'll pay. If you want to ask me out sometime, I'll let you do the honors."

She nodded. "Understood. Ready to speak with my folks?"

"Let's do it."

She held out her palm. "I'll drive. There won't be any shifters around to bother us."

It was her car, and he didn't want her to think he couldn't compromise. He dug his hand in his pocket and retrieved her keys. He thought it cute, but perhaps unwise, that she had four charms dangling from the end of her chain—a sun, a man blowing out wind, a flower, and a boat to indicate water. "Here ya go."

As they left the restaurant, Rye checked the area but detected no shifters, but that didn't mean she was safe by any means. Once at the car, they both slipped inside. She started the engine and then turned to him. "With everything that has happened, I haven't had a chance to spend a lot of time with my folks, so you may have to suffer through a lot of questions."

He grinned. "I can't wait."

A minute later, she pulled into their driveway and cut the engine. "Ready?" she asked.

"As I'll ever be."

Chapter Eight

IZZY SHOULDN'T BE nervous, but she was, and it wasn't because Rye was with her. She feared her overprotective father would insist she move back into their house, and while she'd enjoy their company, Izzy refused to let this creepy Scottish Changeling—if that's what he was—ruin her life. She'd come home to find her family healthy and happy, and she just wanted to enjoy them.

Running into the amazingly attractive Ryerson McKinnon had been wonderful and not what she'd ever imagined. As competent as she was to take care of herself, it was nice to have someone to share her concerns with.

Rye escorted her up to her parents' house, situated only a few acres away from her home. Much larger than her place, the Craftsman style home was majestic and big, but it held a lot of warm memories. She knocked and stepped inside. "Hello?"

Her mom came out of the kitchen with a dishtowel in her hand. "Izzy, I didn't expect you." She looked over at Rye and smiled. "Hello, Ryerson. How was your aura cleansing? I hope my daughter treated you well."

His cheeks dimpled. "It was excellent, thank you. I walked out of there totally refreshed."

For a second, Izzy thought Rye would complain that he'd never received his massage. Perhaps she'd have to schedule one later—when that evil man was no longer a threat.

"Is Dad home?" Izzy asked.

"Yes, he's washing up." Mom turned her head. "Len, Izzy's here," she called upstairs. "Have a seat you two. Can I get you anything to drink?"

"We're good." She glanced at Rye. "Unless you want something?"

"I'm fine." The pressure on her back increased as he led her to the sofa.

Footsteps sounded as her father approached. "Izzy, what a nice surprise, and you brought a friend. What's the occasion?" He gave her a quick hug then shook Rye's hand.

She wasn't sure the best way to begin, so she started right in with her final week in Scotland, and how she felt that someone was watching her. "I didn't mention it before because I didn't want to worry you." She then told them about seeing the wolf and suspecting he was a shifter after she noted the paw prints next to the tire tracks. She left out the part about Naliana contacting her.

"You're safe now that you're home."

She glanced at Rye. "That was what I thought, but a few hours ago, he showed up on my doorstep."

Her mom gasped. "How do you know he's the same man?"

"He told me he was. Mom, he saw me part the sea and make a small windstorm."

Izzy's mother's face paled. "That's not good, Izzy."

"I know, but at the time I wasn't aware he was hiding in the woods spying on me." She explained about wrapping him in a vine and then rushing off to Rye's place. "Exhibiting my skills again might not have been smart, but I feared for my life."

Rye clasped her hand and squeezed it once then let go. "You were right to defend yourself and then come to me."

"From now on, let Rye protect you," her dad said. "We don't need your skills on display unless it's life or death."

"I couldn't agree more." She let out an exasperated breath. "To make it clear, though, I went to Rye's home to ask him his opinion on what I should do, not to protect me. We discussed it and both think this man might come after you both, Missy, or even Teagan."

Her mom glanced at Dad then back at her. "Did he tell you that?"

"No, but he said he wanted something, only I have no idea what that is."

Her dad looked at Rye. "What do you suggest she do?"

"Our hands are tied until he makes his next move. When he does, I want to be there to stop him. I'll come by the spa after Izzy gets off work each day to make sure she gets home safely." Then he told them how this man had attacked him the night before. "He's definitely capable of violence, but next time, I'll be on the lookout for him."

Her first instinct was to object that she didn't need a bodyguard, but it might be nice to see Rye at the end of the day. "What about your job?"

"I'll move my shifts around so I'm free."

"You don't have to do that." Izzy didn't want to be a liability, especially to Rye.

"I want to. My job as an Alpha is to protect."

Part of her heart deflated. Was being with her merely part of his job? The emotional half of her didn't want to believe it.

Her dad nodded. "I'll keep an eye on my family's shop throughout the day."

She didn't need her father to be away from his store. "I can walk next door to let you know we're all good." In reality, she wanted to make sure he was safe since her stalker might be targeting him too. There hadn't been enough time to show them her new enhanced powers, though from her description about how she'd parted the sea, they should be able to guess.

"We'll get through this," her Dad said.

She slapped her thighs and stood. "Well, I've kept Rye away from whatever he needs to be doing long enough. We just wanted to warn you."

Her mom hugged her. "Thank you, sweetheart. You be careful.

I'll call Missy and Teagan tonight and let them know to be watchful too."

"Thanks."

As soon as they left, Izzy debated asking Rye back to her place since they were just next door, but then decided she should take him home. His focus on becoming his father's replacement as Alpha seemed important to him.

Slipping her hand into her purse for her keys, it occurred to her that Rye's lack of car would be a problem. "How are you going to get to town without a car?"

"I'll use my dad's since he's still on vacation."

"It's nice to have family close by, isn't it?" For a second, her eyes watered just remembering how much she'd missed her family these past four years.

"It is."

As she headed down Riverside Drive toward his house, her mind spun, recalling how Rye had stopped to help the motorist, only to be attacked by her stalker and then ended up in a ditch. "I trust you found someone to tow your SUV?"

"Yes. Connor took care of it for me. It should be repaired in a couple of days."

Five minutes later, Izzy pulled into his driveway and cut the engine. She didn't expect him to ask her in—in fact, she wasn't sure she wouldn't make a fool of herself if he did—but she did want to thank him. She reached over and took his hand in hers. "I can't tell you how much I appreciate you having my back today. I have to admit I was a little freaked out when that man showed up out of the blue. In fact, I was so focused on planting the rosebush that I didn't even hear him approach."

Her hands actually shook, surprising even her. He unhooked his seatbelt then leaned over and hugged her. "I'll always be here for you."

When he sat back up, something inside her snapped. She quickly released her seatbelt, leaned over, and drew his face to hers. Then she did what she'd wanted to do for a while—she kissed him. Izzy intended it to be nothing more than a thank you, but the moment their lips touched, every feminine hormone in her body exploded. Sparks burst from her skin and she suspected her blue glow would be evident in the dark of night.

He moaned, and Izzy melted against him. As if Naliana was guiding her, Izzy grabbed his shoulders. That action must have been some kind of signal because the next thing she knew, he was lifting her from her seat, and then sliding her onto his lap all the while keeping their tongues entwined. She should have been embarrassed by her overt display of affection, but she wasn't. Everything about Rye seemed so right and so good.

Go for it.

Her chest constricted for a moment, and it was almost as if the goddess was sending her approval from above.

Rye cupped her face and then broke off the kiss. Both of them were breathing so hard it was as if they'd run a marathon. "You don't know how much I've wanted to do that," Rye said.

"Me too." She didn't comment that she was the one who'd kissed him first. Izzy usually played things cool, calculating her every move, but with Rye, it was easy to let go and be herself.

His hand roamed over to her breast, and in that instant, she wanted more. If she hadn't been sitting on his lap she might have even grabbed his crotch. Desire flooded her system and she needed to taste him again. He hadn't asked her inside his place, and she didn't want to push her luck. Playing high school teenagers in the front seat of her car wasn't her thing, but right now, she was in the most perfect place—sitting on Ryerson McKinnon's lap.

"Touch me more," she whispered.

Rye's growl came from deep within his chest. "I want to make you come."

Those words had her sagging against him. "Don't let me stop you."

"You drive me wild, witchy woman."

Izzy laughed at her nickname and dragged her lips over his. She inhaled his musky scent and it blended with the hint of wine they'd had at dinner. Needing more contact, she lifted his shirt from his pants and slid her fingers underneath. This time, she groaned at the feel of his muscle-packed chest underneath his soft pad of fur.

"You aren't going to go all animal on me, are you?" she asked, fearing he was about to shift.

"If you keep touching me that way, I might."

Wolves were beautiful creatures, but only at a distance—except, of course, if it was Rye. Growing up, she'd never had the honor of seeing him in his wolf form, but she could imagine he'd be regal and imposing.

As she explored higher on his chest, Rye slid his hand between her legs and cupped her mound. Her body instantly caught fire. And here, she thought she was the only one who could set something ablaze with a flick of the wrist. Rye was more talented than she was.

Acting as if he was afraid of spooking her, he slowly slid his hand to her waistband. When she didn't stop him, he unhooked the button then pulled down her zipper. That motion alone drove her crazy with anticipation.

The moment his fingers parted her folds, Izzy nearly climaxed. She clutched his pecs and then nibbled on his lip, his chin, and finally the spot between his throat and his shoulder. His scent invaded her body and contractions rumbled inside her. How was this man able to turn her on to the point where she'd do anything to have his cock? His erection was like a steel pipe and Izzy had to adjust her position for more comfort. If his finger hadn't slipped into her wet hole just then, she would have straddled him despite there being no room in her car. As it was, she had to bend over or chance banging her head on the roof.

Rye curled his finger, and when he hit her most sensitive spot, she practically yelled out his name to take her. She lifted her head and gulped in some much needed oxygen. When he added a second finger, she lost it, and her climax swooped down on her, sending sparks shimmying up her spine.

After nearly losing feeling in her fingers, she finally let up on the pressure she had on his shoulders. Gouging him had never been part of her plan.

"Oh, my," she gasped.

Rye slipped his fingers out of her and the sudden emptiness made her ache. He moaned as he licked them clean. "You taste like heaven. I want you so badly, but you've been through a lot today, and I don't want to pressure you." With that, he eased her off his lap. "I'd ask you in, but I don't trust myself around you, and I won't rush us into anything. It has been a long day for you, and I suggest a hot bath to relax. I will definitely be thinking of you tonight my beautiful witchy woman."

"Okay." That was a stupid comment as there hadn't been any pressure on his part, but if she told him she wanted to make love with him, it might hurt their tentative relationship. Clearly, he was confused too.

In what seemed like a last second decision, Rye cupped the back of her head and kissed her with more passion than he'd ever shown before. Confusion rushed through her again. What kind of man would bring a woman to climax and then stop? A noble one, she suspected.

Rye was right though. Today had been harrowing, and she needed time to figure out what she wanted to do.

"I'll see you after work tomorrow," she said.

He smiled. "I'll be there."

With that, he jumped out of her car. As soon as he stepped inside, Izzy took off, not wanting to be tempted to pound on his door and demand he make love with her. On the way back to her house, her entire body vibrated. By the time she pulled into the driveway, she had a grin on her face wider than the Grand Canyon.

AS SOON AS Rye stepped inside his house, he plastered his back against the wall. What the fuck had he been thinking? Izzy must think he was some sex-craved lunatic. She had to be reeling from finding out that some Scottish loon was after her, and yet he'd fingered her in the front seat of her car, something he hadn't done since sophomore year in high school.

Disgusted with himself, he grabbed a beer then called Kalan in the hopes he wasn't still at work.

His Beta answered after the first ring. "Yo, what's up?"

"I have a situation I need to discuss with you."

"It sounds serious."

"It is. Do you mind stopping over?"

"Be right there." Kalan then disconnected.

Before Rye finished half the bottle, his best friend knocked then entered. Rye nodded to the fresh beer on the counter then walked over to the sofa and propped his feet up on the table. "We had an incident today. Two actually."

"We?"

"Izzy and me." He told Kalan about her stalker and how she'd used her magic to secure the man before running over to his place. "She was really shaken, so we went back to her place to check on the man, but he'd escaped. Over dinner we decided this creep might come at her through her parents so we stopped over there to warn them."

"Do you think this was the same man who ran you off the road?"

"The man who came to Izzy's said he'd seen her perform her magic in Scotland. What are the chances there are two Scots in town?"

"Slim. What would you like me to do?"

"If I had a photo of him, I'd suggest we put his face all over town, but we don't have one yet. Izzy confirmed he was about five feet ten or eleven inches, lacked muscle tone, had auburn hair, a thin nose, and pale skin."

Kalan tossed back his beer. "He sounds hard to miss. After he stabbed you, I asked the others to keep an eye out for someone with a Scottish accent. Having his description should help." He leaned forward. "You said there were two things. What was the other?"

"I'm ashamed to admit this, but after she drove me home, Izzy leaned over and kissed me. It was probably her way of saying thank you."

Kalan's brows rose. "Why would that be shameful? Sounds like a great thing to me."

"Because that one kiss turned into something else."

His friend laughed. "Don't tell me you did the dirty?"

"No, but I was this close." He held his thumb and forefinger a half inch apart.

Shaking his head, Kalan set the bottle on the coffee table in front of him and leaned back. "I bet when you stopped it pissed her off."

Rye hoped not. "I explained myself."

"You are a piece of work. What are you waiting for? She's your mate."

"That is exactly why I want to give her time to get used to me. I can't afford to mess this up."

"When are you going to see her next?"

"Tomorrow." He explained how he needed to make certain she arrived home safely. "I don't trust that ass not to follow her again."

"What makes you think he's not at her house now? If I'd been tied up in a vine, I might want a second chance at her."

"Oh, shit." Rye's blood nearly boiled. He jumped up and raced to his phone then set it down. "I don't have her number."

"Then call Mrs. Berta and ask her for it."

"Good idea." Rye wasn't thinking clearly. He dialed Izzy's mom, and when she answered, he explained that he needed to ask Izzy something but didn't know her cell number. Telling her mom the whole truth might cause more issues. He considered asking her dad to check on her, but what could Mr. Berta do against a werewolf?

She gave him the needed information. "Thank you for being so good to my daughter."

"You're welcome." If he'd been truly good, he would have

checked her house out first before having her drive him home. He glanced over at Kalan. "Got it."

Just as he was about to punch in the number, he wondered if Izzy would be upset that he doubted her ability to take care of herself considering she'd told him numerous times how competent she was.

"What are you waiting for?" Kalan asked.

"I don't want her to think I'm hovering."

Kalan picked up his beer and tipped it back. "Why would she think that? Her stalker stabbed you for fuck's sake. If he's good enough to do that to someone who's trained to hear every crunch of stone, think what he could do to Izzy."

Rye dragged a hand over his head. "You're right. If I thought she'd say yes, I'd ask her to stay here." He dialed her number, trying to think of what to say.

"Hello?" She sounded out of breath as if she'd run to answer the phone. Shit. In the background, water was running, probably in the tub. An intense visual formed in his mind's eye.

"Izzy, hey it's me, Rye. I wanted to make sure you didn't get any more surprises when you arrived home."

"Aw. That is sweet of you to call, but it's all clear here."

The churning in his stomach lessened. "Great. I just wanted to check. I'll see you tomorrow then. You have my number now, so call if you need me."

She chuckled. "I will. Good night, Rye."

The image of her naked in the tub kept flashing in his mind, forcing him to hang up quickly. He couldn't tell if she appreciated the call or thought he was being too overprotective. He ran his hands through his hair, needing a moment to compose himself.

"So?" Kalan asked. There was way too much humor in his tone.

"All's good."

Kalan waved his beer. "I've never seen you like this before."

"Like what?"

"Unsure of yourself and second-guessing your every move. That's not very Alpha-like behavior."

If anyone other than Kalan had said that, it would have been a reason to shift and fight. "This whole mate thing has thrown me for a loop. When she told me how that Scotsman had stepped foot on Wendayan land and threatened her, I lost it."

"You felt helpless."

That was a good word for it. "Yes, and I didn't like it one bit. That's why I'm going to take her home tomorrow after work and stay for as long as she lets me."

Kalan grinned. "Just don't bite her when you make love."

His stupid pulse soared at the idea. "We aren't to that stage yet."

"Sure." Kalan stood then set his bottle on the counter. "Let me know how that goes."

Rye gave him the finger, and they both laughed. As soon as Kalan left, Rye headed to the shower, needing a real cold one tonight.

Chapter Nine

WHEN IZZY WENT into work the next day, she was still glowing from Rye's kiss and amazing touches—and from the phone call. Rye checking up on her meant a lot to her. Until she showed him her extensive control over the elements, she'd have to go along with his protective nature.

She wasn't so naïve to believe that she was invincible. Last night, when she'd pulled into her driveway, she'd carefully looked around before leaving her car, fearing that creep might have come back. Yes, she could have asked her dad to come over to check out the place with her, but then she decided she could summon the wind to push her stalker away. Her father would have used fire and probably scorched the hair off the man's head. She never realized how talented her father was until she'd tried to mimic his precision—and failed.

Izzy parked in front of the spa just a few minutes before it was to open. The storefront window hadn't changed much since before she'd left to study in Europe. Hell, she bet her mom hadn't even switched out the candles or the crystals in all that time. Good thing Mom didn't run a clothing store or everything would be out of style. In the long run, if the display brought in customers, that was all that mattered.

When she stepped inside, both Missy and Teagan rushed up to her.

Missy threw her arms around her first. "Mom told us what happened. You should have called me. Do you really think that guy will come after us?" She stepped back.

After hugging Teagan, Izzy walked behind the counter and placed her purse and keys in the cabinet. "I wish I knew. He wants something, but I have no idea what it is. I fear that if I don't give it to him, he might use one or all of you to get to me."

Missy and Teagan looked at each other. "I don't sense any evil hovering nearby," Teagan said. "If I do, I'll be sure to let you know."

"I'd appreciate it." Teagan's ability to foreshadow the future had just come into full power from what Missy had told her and seemed fairly accurate. Knowing that Teagan would watch out for them made Izzy feel a little better. The tension in her sister's face lessened too. "But just in case, be on the lookout for someone who looks obviously Scottish. He won't be wearing a kilt, but his auburn hair and pale skin will make him stand out."

"Thanks. We'll be keeping an eye out for him," Missy said. "Speaking of men, Mom said you brought Rye over to the house. What's up with that?" A shine glinted in her eye.

"Don't look at me like that. There's nothing going on." Yet. Too bad the words came out slowly, implying she was trying to formulate a lie.

"Uh-huh. Why were you with him then?"

"When that Scotsman showed up at my house, I feared he might harm me, so I wrapped him in a vine then rushed over to Rye's place. I figured he would know what to do."

Teagan glanced to the ceiling and inhaled. "Did Rye wrap his arms around you and tell you not to worry—that everything would be okay?"

Izzy laughed at their antics. "No, but just so you know, he's insisting on following me home for a few days to make sure I'm safe—or until we catch this guy."

The girls shot a knowing glance at each other. Fortunately, the bell above the door rang and saved her from any further discussion. An older woman she didn't recognize came in.

Missy rushed up to her, chatted, and then escorted her to one of the rooms in back. Four years ago, Izzy had known everyone around here. Now, it seemed as if she was a stranger in her own hometown.

Izzy leaned against the counter while Teagan straightened the candles, lotions, and crystals on the shelves on the far wall. "Missy wrote that you and Kip are dating. How's that going?" Kip Landon was another Wendayan, and while he was a few years older than Teagan, Izzy was happy they were together. They seemed like a good match.

"We are, but we want to take it slowly." Teagan faced her. "Don't get me wrong. The sex is out of this world. I'm mean when we're together, the whole room seems to be cast in blue, but let's say we conflict over how I handle my visions."

For some reason, that didn't feel like the real reason they hadn't mated. "Are you intimidated by his powers? Is that it?"

"Me? No. I mean he can control things like electric motors and anything to do with power. I've even seen him shoot electricity out of his palm that I bet could fry a person."

"That talent is nothing to sneeze about."

"I agree, but I'm learning to move items with my mind, and I think my lack of control bothers him."

So that was the crux of the conflict. "He said that? That your talents bother him?"

Teagan glanced to the side. "Not in so many words."

"Back up a minute. Can you really move things with your mind?"

Teagan nodded. "Yes, and I discovered it by accident." She glanced at the ceiling and a sparkle came to her eyes. "We were fooling around, and I was so excited that I swiped my hand in the air, and a book flew across the room and nearly hit Kip!"

"Wow."

"It happened again one other time, only then I was angry."

Her heightened emotions seemed to be causing the added abilities. "Can you move things at will?"

"So far, I've succeeded with only small items, and even then, I can't even move them far, but I'm working to improve my skills."

Stunned, Izzy pushed off from the counter and moved closer. "Show me."

No one was in the street to see her, so Teagan nodded. "I'll move this tea candle."

Izzy might be able to control the forces of nature, which in affect was moving things like vines, sand, and wind, but when she'd attempted to move a glass across a table, she'd completely failed.

Teagan narrowed her eyes as if she were focusing some kind of projected light beam on the object. Seconds later, the tea candle moved an inch. Her cousin's shoulders dropped, and she faced Izzy with a grin on her face. "It wasn't much, but I'm getting better every day."

"That's fantastic. And you say Kip's not supportive?"

"He says he is, but I'm not sure he's really happy about it."

Izzy nodded, but she was convinced there was more to the story. "Men definitely have egos."

"Amen."

Another customer came in wanting to purchase some crystals, and Teagan took care of her. Feeling unneeded, Izzy motioned she was going next door to her dad's cell phone store to make sure he was okay. When she entered, two people were wandering around checking out the different phones while her dad was helping another customer. She waved to him and he held up his finger for her to wait. When it became evident that his conversation would take a while, she smiled, waved, and returned to the spa, happy her father was fine.

For the rest of the day, Izzy rang up customers and checked on her dad, but each time he was busy with someone. At the spa, she was called upon to give one massage, and that was when Teagan and Missy were busy.

All in all, her day kind of sucked. Not only did she wonder about her stalker, she had hoped Rye would have called to make sure the Scotsman hadn't stopped by. If nothing else, he could have asked how she was holding up since her incident. Most likely Rye didn't want to be a pest.

About ten minutes before he was due to pick her up, she wanted to check on her father once more. This time when she entered his store, the place was empty.

"Hey," she said. "You're actually free!"

"It has been a busy day, but it's time to close up shop. Mom called and wants me to take her out to dinner."

"Nice."

"Mind doing me a favor?"

"Not at all," she said happy to be useful.

"I didn't have anyone in here for about a half hour so I shredded some documents. Do you mind emptying the trash while I close out the cash register? The two large bags of material are by the back door.

"No problem." Izzy stepped to the back, picked them up, and headed out to the alley. The dumpster was located at the end of the strip mall past the spa.

Despite the alley being unpaved, the air smelled sweet and the breeze made the temperature nearly perfect. As she neared the dumpster, someone stepped out from behind it, and her heart nearly jumped out of her body.

It was *him*. Shit. All she could think of was that this stalker was within a few feet of her sister, cousin, and dad. At the moment, they were the only two people in the alley, but hopefully that would change shortly.

"What do you want?" she asked then set down her two bags.

The asshole smiled. "I want you."

Was he out of his mind? He slowly advanced and goose bumps peppered her skin. Izzy debated on what to use to stop him. Should it be wind or fire? She held out her hand to shoot a fireball at his feet, but nothing happened. She jerked her hand again and concentrated hard as she tried once more. Again, she failed.

"Oh my sweet, Isadora, not so powerful anymore, are you?" he said with a disgusting amount of cheer.

Blood pounded in her ears, and her stomach tumbled. She didn't understand why her powers weren't working or how it was even possible. Izzy held her palm parallel to the ground in an attempt to create a whirlwind, but she couldn't even make the dirt move at her feet. Frantic, she swept her arms around to create a wind strong enough to blow him over, but her abilities still eluded her.

"Help!" Izzy's shout came out weak. She turned and ran back toward her father's store. In a flash, the horrid man was on her, a hand clamped over her mouth.

"You're coming with me, lass. The more you struggle, the worse it will be for you."

To hell it would be. Izzy had never known such helplessness before. She kicked him in the shin and tried to elbow him in the gut, but nothing seemed to affect him. With his hand squeezing her jaw, she couldn't scream out again. Oh, why couldn't she have inherited the ability to communicate telepathically?

As he dragged her past the Crystal Winds Spa, the back door opened and Teagan appeared. "Izzy!" she shouted then immediately shot back inside.

"Fuck," her captor said.

Knowing that someone had seen this man trying to capture her gave Izzy a burst of hope until she realized that even if Teagan called the sheriff's department, it would take too long to respond.

She lifted both of her feet in an attempt to create more drag and delay her capture, but then the man covered her nose, probably in retaliation. "I'll carry you if I have to," he said. From his heavy breathing, dragging her along was taking its toll.

"Put her down." The command came from behind them.

Rye! She nearly cried with relief.

Izzy lifted her hand to jab her captor in the eye, but hit his shoulder instead. Just then, the back door to her father's store opened and he rushed out. Teagan must have called him. Dad charged and growls sounded behind her.

Next thing she knew, she was on the ground gasping for breath.

Her dad reached her first. "You okay, honey?"

"I will be." She twisted around to see what was happening. Teeth bared, two wolves were battling it out, and two sets of torn clothes were strewn in the middle of the fray.

She recognized her stalker as the wolf she'd seen at the seaside with the white spot on his forehead and gray fur. Only now his eyes were glowing red. The other animal was truly magnificent. His muzzle was white sprinkled with gray, but the rest of his sleek body was a blend of white, black, and gold.

Rye's wolf snarled and swiped a claw across her stalker's face. The Changeling wolf yelped and shot past Rye, running down the alley. Rye turned to go after him, but then stopped. He rushed up to her.

"I'm okay," she said.

Rye howled and rubbed up against her leg. His caress helped take away some of the pain radiating through her. She squatted in front of him and ran her hand down his sleek back. His bristles were so soft and comforting. "Thank you."

Rye nuzzled his head under her hand, and she stroked him again then scratched behind his ears. The back door to the spa opened, and Teagan rushed out. Her gaze shot to the wolf, and she slowed.

"It's okay. It's Rye. He saved me."

Teagan advanced. "Are you okay?"

"Thanks to you and Rye."

Her father stepped next to the wolf. "How about getting a robe for Rye, Teagan? Or better yet, Rye, why don't you follow Teagan in. You can cover up in the spa."

The whole concept of Rye being naked once he returned to his human form had heat racing up her face. Right now, that was the least of her worries, however. Izzy looked down the alley, but her stalker was nowhere in sight. At least, he'd have to run home. Changing back into his human form might prove embarrassing and cause another call to the sheriff's department.

Izzy stood and inhaled a deep breath then dusted herself off, but she couldn't stop shaking.

Rye's wolf stepped back and glanced up at Teagan who pointed toward the door. "Sure thing. Come on… Rye."

"Wait!" Izzy spotted his keys and wallet on the ground and gathered his torn clothes. "He'll need these."

Teagan stepped down and collected his gear. "What about the other stuff?"

Izzy's father moved next to her. "We'll dispose of them. The man might have left some identification."

Teagan nodded and held the door open for Rye.

Her father wrapped an arm around Izzy's waist. "Come back to the store."

"No, I need to go home." She turned to Rye who was halfway inside. "Rye, meet me at my place."

He let out a soft woof, and she took that as a yes. Izzy turned to go back with her dad when she nearly tripped over the two bags of shredded papers. "Sorry, I never got to dump these."

"That's the least of our worries. What happened back there?"

She stepped inside his store and set down the bags. The enormity of losing her powers and being attacked hit her like an eighteen-wheeler truck. "I don't know. Suddenly, my powers wouldn't work. It was as if being around that man altered something inside me."

"They worked the first time."

"I know."

When she spotted some paper on his counter, Izzy rushed over to it and held her hand over them and tried to send a puff of wind under it, but it remained still. Her heart pounded faster than a jackhammer. "I don't understand."

Her dad engulfed her in a big hug and patted her back. "There has to be a reason. I'll drive you home. Maybe your mother can help figure it out."

"I appreciate that, but I can drive, Dad. How about I follow you?"

"I'll follow you."

She didn't see the difference, unless he feared that maniac would try to run her off the road or something. "Okay. What do you think we should do to stop this crazy person?"

"Rye's Beta is a deputy. I'll speak with him."

"Thank you." She nodded to the odious man's clothes. "Is his wallet in there?"

Her dad stuck his hand in the pants pockets. "Nothing."

"So he must have left his keys and wallet in his car then."

Her dad shrugged. "Perhaps he kept the car running, thinking that he'd have to dump you in the trunk or something."

Every muscle in her body turned heavy. "This is worse than I ever imagined."

"It will all work out. You're safe now."

Until she left her house again. Hell, what would stop that lunatic from returning there right now? Chills rippled down her spine. Rye! Maybe she should ask him not to head on over there.

Not only would Rye never back down, if he'd bested that creep the first time, he could do it again. "Can we go now? I don't want Rye to wait too long."

"Sure, honey."

Once her father locked up, he followed her until he turned off at his place. She honked, waved, and drove to her driveway.

When she arrived, Rye was leaning against the truck—fully clothed—and she nearly cried with joy that he was safe and that loathsome man wasn't around. Rye had saved her. Never again would she be so arrogant to think that she couldn't use help. Having him near was like someone with wings holding her up by the shoulders. Izzy pulled up next to him and slipped out.

On her first step, her knees gave way and she had to grab the car handle. A second later, Rye was by her side.

"Let's get you inside." He swooped her up and carried her down the path. Under normal circumstances, she would have demanded he put her down, but right now, she needed to be in his arms.

At the door, he set her down so she could open up. As she

stepped in, Rye held out a hand for her to stop then glanced around. Fear jammed a spike down her throat. "You don't think he'd be in here do you?"

"No, I'd sense him if he were, but I like to be cautious. Why don't you sit down, and I'll get you something to drink."

That sounded wonderful. While she normally wasn't the type to let a man take care of her, she was so distraught that she needed time to regroup. "How about a glass of wine? I need something stronger than tea or water."

"You got it."

Rye disappeared into the kitchen. Cabinets banged and drawers opened. If she'd had the strength, she would have helped him.

"Wine's in the caddy next to the fridge," she called out.

"Found it." He returned a minute later with two glasses of wine then sat next to her. "Tell me exactly what happened."

Chapter Ten

O WEN WAS SEETHING mad. To be bested by that punk ate away at his very being. Rye would pay.

He closed the trunk of his car and jumped in the driver's seat, careful to make sure no one had seen him. It was why he'd parked next to the alley. Thank goodness he was forward thinking and had a spare set of clothes in his car just for such an emergency. To think he went to all the trouble of binding Isadora's powers only to leave empty handed. He wouldn't give up though. He would have Isadora Berta as his wife, no matter what.

Pulling onto the main drag, he headed north toward the mountains, anger setting his veins on fire. Failed. Again. It was Scotland all over again. He'd been destined to be Alpha of his Clan, and if hadn't been for Shamus MacLeod, Owen would have led his Changelings to victory. It wasn't his fault that someone had leaked his whereabouts.

His parents were embarrassed by the defeat and said he wasn't settled enough to lead so they stripped him of his future title and gave it to his younger brother who was mated. They felt the Clan's Changelings would listen to a man with commitments and priorities. Owen would just have to prove to them that he could be that man. When he returned with his new wife whose magic was unsurpassed, they would change their minds.

As for his beautiful mate, he almost wished he hadn't gone to the square that day and been stunned by her beauty. Almost, but not quite. She might a lot of trouble, but in the end it would be worth it.

Alpha Owen Chancellor had such a nice ring to it.

As MUCH AS Izzy didn't want to relive that horrible event, she needed someone with a level head to help her understand how she'd lost her powers. That evil man had to have had an effect on her somehow, and since both he and Rye were werewolves, she hoped Rye could give her some insight.

Izzy sipped her wine. "I'd finished work and decided to check up on dad. Because he wanted to leave a bit early, he asked if I'd take out the trash. Halfway to the dumpster, my stalker jumped out from behind the bin and came toward me."

"Why didn't you stop him?"

The humiliation made her stomach sick. "I tried, but my powers had inexplicably disappeared." Her voice shook as it trailed off.

Rye stilled. "I don't understand. How is that possible?"

"I don't know."

He looked around. "Show me. Try to move those papers on the desk like you did before."

Izzy sniffled and then stood. Rye seemed to have so much confidence in her that maybe her abilities had been affected because of her fear. With Rye nearby, she knew that nothing would happen to her. At the desk, she held her hand over the paper and concentrated of summoning the air to swirl. She then lifted her arm but nothing happened. "I could do this by the time I was five," she said, choking out a sob.

Rye came over to her. "Come sit back down. Hopefully, it's temporary."

She spun to face him. "Don't patronize me. Something has happened, and I need to find out what it is." Her damn voice squeaked, sounding shrill.

He held up his hands. "Okay. What do you want to do?"

She didn't know. "Maybe only my abilities to shoot fire and create wind are messed up. I'm hoping that I was just so scared that when that stalker showed up, my abilities shut down. I'd like to try something else, and I feel the most creative by the falls.

"Are you afraid now?"

"No, but—"

"I get it." Rye motioned toward the door. "Let's go check it out."

She hesitated, wondering if she failed whether Rye's opinion of her would change for the worse. "I'll go by myself if you don't mind."

He lowered his chin. "Ain't going to happen."

While his tone wasn't harsh, he didn't seem willing to give in. "Fine, but you'll have to sit quietly while I do my thing."

Rye cupped her face, and all bad thoughts flew from her mind. "I will do anything I can to help you."

His sincerity helped lower her anxiety. "Thank you."

After locking up, Rye escorted her down the path that led to the twenty-foot tall waterfall. Because this was on Wendayan property, it was secluded—a place to practice without the humans finding out about any secret talents.

The pines, oaks, and maples were thick and full leading up the waterfall. Surrounding the base were mountain laurels and rhododendron. In June, when they bloomed, the area was awash with pink and white flowers. A few hundred feet past the falls sat the ten-acre Cove Lake.

She led him past the falls to the lake's edge where she'd practiced many times before. A rock outcropping sat to the east. Rye climbed on top and sat, saying nothing. His willingness to give her space helped settle her. Being able to concentrate and not having to worry about that creep sneaking up on her was invaluable.

Perhaps she would start with one of the first things she'd learned as a child, which was to make a plant grow merely by lifting her arm above it. Standing next to a weed, she bent over, lowered her hand to hover, and then raised it as she stood up. The plant barely moved in the wind. "Let me try that again," she mumbled.

Izzy attempted the feat several more times, working with weeds first and then some ferns. With each failed attempt, her stomach churned.

Rye eased up off the rock and came over to her. "Why don't we grab something to eat and you can try again later."

She hated failure, but nothing more could be accomplished right now. "That sounds good."

She must have looked totally dejected because he drew her into a hug. "It's going to be okay."

She leaned back. "How do you know that? Everything was going so well until that creep came into my life."

"We'll sort this out. I asked Kalan to put everyone on the lookout for this man. As soon as I tell him what happened, the department can arrest him for attempted kidnapping."

She sucked in a breath. "You can't tell him."

His brows pinched. "Why not?"

Because I'm embarrassed. Think... She did want that man caught. "Can you tell Kalan everything but my failed abilities to stop the man?"

A small smile lifted his lips. "You bet."

Rye was so wonderful that she wanted to blanket herself in his comfort and goodness. Whether it was just to thank him again or because she needed to have his lips on hers, she drew his head down and kissed him.

The moment their mouths touched, her insides exploded, and an unintentional moan escaped as small blue sparks shimmered on her skin. Most were lopsided and faded quickly as if the binding had affected that too. At least what she was feeling was just as strong as ever, if not more so.

Standing next to the waterfall encased by nature had soothed her nerves, and she drank in his protectiveness. Whether it was the horror of the day or the fear that her magical life was over, Izzy wanted Rye inside her. No one ever came to this private area, so they wouldn't be disturbed. If by chance her stalker reappeared, Rye would sense him.

She leaned back and lifted his torn fire department T-shirt from his pants.

Hair instantaneously sprouted on his face, and his eyes changed to a golden-green hue. "You sure? You've been through a lot."

She huffed out a chuckle. "Are you trying to talk *me* out of this, or yourself?"

"Not me." He lifted her up by her butt until their lips were level. Then he kissed her with an intense passion that convinced her he was telling the truth. They both opened their mouths at the same time and his tongue delved into her mouth. He tasted like mint, as if he'd cleaned up before he'd come to follow her home.

She wrapped her legs around his waist and felt his erection press against her. As much as she wanted to control all the forces of nature, she wanted Rye more. Needing to touch his skin, she lowered her legs and unbuttoned his jeans. Her eyes opened wide. "Whoa. I didn't expect commando."

"I only had jeans, this torn shirt, and a pair of old boots in the car."

He sure wore those old clothes well, but he'd look better without them. "I want you, Rye."

His Adam's apple bobbed. "I want you too. More than you can ever know."

As if making love with him would reconnect her to her powers, she lowered his jeans to his hips, bent over, and pulled his big cock toward her. She inhaled then licked him from bottom to top.

Rye hissed and grabbed a handful of her hair. "I'm on the edge. Better be fast."

Izzy drew him deep into her throat and swirled her tongue around his wide shaft. Suddenly, Rye stepped back and buttoned up his pants.

Disappointment swamped her. "What happened? Didn't you like it?"

"We have company."

Her heart dropped to her stomach. Izzy spun around, expecting *him*—only it was Ophelia Eastwood—a Wendayan witch. "Ophelia, what are you doing here?"

"Your mother was worried about you."

Izzy blew out a breath. Of course, her mom would consult her favorite witch. Stooped shoulders and straggly white hair, Ophelia had to be close to ninety if she was a day. She was not only wise; her talent with spells was extensive.

"Thank you, but I'm fine."

Ophelia moved closer. "Don't lie to me."

Shit. She didn't need this. All Izzy wanted was to get lost in Rye's warmth. "I'm sorry. Okay, I'm not fine. I lost my powers today, and I'm trying to reconnect with them."

The witch raised one brow, and a smile flitted across her face. She then sobered. Holding out her hands, she hummed one note. With her eyes closed, she waved her arms. "You have a black aura about you."

Her heart lurched. "A black aura?"

Rye touched Izzy's arm. "What does that mean?" he whispered.

The witch answered instead. "It seems Isadora's powers were bound by someone who did not have her best interest at heart."

The breath whooshed out of her. Someone had put a spell on her, and she didn't need a degree in science to know who had ordered it—that motherfucking Scotsman. "You can reverse this spell, right?"

"I'm afraid not."

Izzy leaned into Rye who wrapped an arm around her waist. "There must be something I can do." Her entire identity was wrapped up in her abilities.

"Let the spell run its course. I've not seen anything like this in years, but these things shouldn't last more than forty-eight hours."

Her pulse slowed. "What if this witch puts another spell on me?"

Ophelia shook her head. "She can't. Not right away at least. Spells need a twenty-four hour renewal period."

That gave her some solace. "I appreciate the information."

Knowing this horror would end soon, the tension in her shoulders eased.

"Sorry to have interrupted you." Ophelia turned around and seemed to disappear into the light.

Izzy looked up at Rye. As much as she wanted to continue where they'd left off, now wasn't the right time. "I guess I have to wait, but forty-eight hours seems a long time."

"We haven't exhausted all of our resources."

"If you're thinking of pleading to Naliana, it won't work. She didn't respond the last time I tried to contact her."

"I was thinking of James."

Her husband? The man was a recluse. "You know him?"

"He lives on the other side of the lake, and because it's not a white moon, he won't be entertaining Naliana."

She'd always been fascinated by James—or rather the lore surrounding him. "You've actually met Naliana's husband?"

He chuckled. "A few times."

"Isn't he supposed to be hundreds of years old?"

"So I've heard, but I can attest to the fact that the man hasn't aged for as long as I've known him. Dad says the same thing."

"He's an immortal?"

"Apparently."

She'd never met one before. For the first time since she'd lost her powers, hope surged through her. "Can we go now?"

Rye ran a knuckle down her cheek. "You don't want to eat first?"

"Hell, no."

RYE WASN'T SURE what to expect as they walked up to James's cabin, but he wouldn't be deterred. Izzy's situation was dire. Poor woman. Rye couldn't imagine what she was going through. If the circumstances had been reversed and he'd lost his ability to shift, he sure as hell wouldn't have remained so calm.

Before he was able to raise his hand to knock, the door opened.

"Rye, good to see you. And who do we have here?"

"This is Izzy Berta. She's a—"

His eyes shone. "A Wendayan. Yes, you're Kathryn's daughter. Why you look just like your mom. Come in."

Izzy's eyes went wide, as if her mom had never mentioned it. With a hand to Izzy's back, Rye led her into the rather sparse stone cabin. A fireplace dominated the home, but it wasn't lit due to the warm summer temperatures. No kitchen was evident, but he suspected it was located down the hall. James's furniture appeared to have been handcrafted from local hardwoods, possibly made around the turn of the last century, and upholstered cushions graced the sofa and chair.

"May I get you something to drink? From the look on your faces, you could use a strong one. Ale perhaps?"

While Rye might like one, he doubted Izzy would. "Have any wine?"

"I'll check."

As soon as James disappeared down a corridor, Izzy leaned into Rye. "He's not at all how I pictured him."

"You're thinking he would look more like Ophelia?"

"Yes. James looks vital. Sure his hair is gray, but other than that he seems quite fit."

"I agree." If he didn't know the man was immortal, he would have pegged him to be around sixty.

James returned with three glasses of wine on a tray. "Drink up and tell me what troubles you. If you came here for relationship advice, I'm afraid you'll have to wait until Naliana returns."

"No," she said. "I'm being stalked." Izzy glanced at Rye and then began her tale of being followed in Scotland, how Naliana had called her home, and then how that same man had followed her to Silver Lake. She went on to explain that a few hours ago, he'd attacked her in the alley behind her work and that suddenly her powers were gone. "Ophelia said that a black aura had been cast over me."

"I'm so sorry, my dear. You must have been very frightened, not only at being assaulted but from losing something so dear to you."

She clasped Rye's hand. "I was."

"Did the man say what he wanted?"

"No, only that he wasn't leaving without it."

James looked over at Rye. "Could he be a Changeling?"

"I'm assuming he is, but in all honesty, I don't know how their system works in Scotland. However, he was able to get a witch to cast a spell."

James tipped back his drink. "Let me see what I can do. I have a few connections. Leave your cell number, and I'll be in contact. I'll also find out if Naliana has anything to add."

Izzy leaned forward. "I can't thank you enough. Anything you do will be much appreciated."

They chatted a bit while they finished their wine then said their goodbyes. Once back in Rye's truck, Izzy twisted toward him. "Do you think he can help?"

"I don't know, but James will try his best. I have no idea what kind of connections he was referring to, but I'm sure he's made many friends over the years, and probably a few enemies too."

As Rye headed back into town for something to eat, Izzy called her mother to tell her what Ophelia Eastwood had said. To his surprise, she didn't mention their visit to James. She must have believed he'd want her to keep quiet, though her mom and James did seem to know each other.

After they ate, Rye wanted to discuss something that had been on his mind. He wasn't sure Izzy would go along with it, but if she did agree, losing her powers for two days might be the least of her worries.

Chapter Eleven

IZZY FIGURED WAITING another day or so before her powers returned wouldn't be so horrible now that the sheriff's department was searching for that creep, and Naliana's husband was looking into it. She suspected the Scotsman would be found and brought to justice quite soon.

Rye had suggested they stop at Nate's Pizzeria, claiming he didn't want to spend too much time eating. Part of her was disappointed he wanted to rush back because she enjoyed being with him, but she understood he was probably concerned for her safety.

Between the two of them, they managed to eat two pizzas. Totally full, he drove her home, but she refused to let fear enter her head. To stave off her anxiety, she wanted to make a suggestion that Rye might not like.

He pulled into her driveway and faced her. "Please hear me out before you say no," he said.

She hadn't expected that comment. From what she could remember, she'd been quite accommodating. She debated asking if she could speak first, but his serious demeanor had her holding her tongue. "Okay."

"Until this maniac is caught, I want you to stay with me."

Izzy almost chuckled at Rye's tight jaw and lifted chin. "Actually, I was going to suggest something along those lines as well. Only I was going to see if you'd be willing to stay at my place."

The tension in his face evaporated. Rye picked up her hands and lifted them to his lips. "Thank you for understanding, but my house is safer. If your stalker is a Changeling, then his powers will be diminished if he steps foot in our compound."

"I didn't realize that. I guess I can always ask my parents to keep an eye out on my place and let me know if that creep shows. Knowing Dad, he won't have any issues with tossing a fireball at him."

Rye chuckled. "He doesn't need to go that far, though far be it for me to stop him."

Both of their homes were equally close to town, so her commute wouldn't change. Since most of the shifter population lived around the lake, if this man ever tried to snatch her again, she bet the wolf and bear shifters would help. "I guess I need to pack then."

His smile made her want a repeat performance in the front seat of his car, but if he pulled away again, she'd have to retaliate—when her powers returned.

"Sounds good," Rye said.

He insisted on checking out her house again before he let her inside. It was over-the-top, but his siblings ran a security company, so he must have picked up some paranoia as well as a few pointers from them.

"Everything good?" she asked.

"Yes."

Figuring they could return to her house for more clothes whenever she needed, Izzy packed for only a couple of days.

"What about all your crystals and stuff?" Rye called from the living room.

How thoughtful that he asked. "They stay, since Mom's been using this house for her special clients," she called back—meaning those like the McKinnons and the Murdochs. She might treat some others here, but she'd never asked.

Izzy packed a few outfits and toiletries then returned to the living room.

"That's all you need?" he asked.

She laughed. "I only took two suitcases with me when I moved to Europe."

He smiled then lifted the case from her fingers. The action didn't imply he believed she wasn't incapable of carrying it, but more of a gentleman thing. Because she didn't want to be without her own transportation, she followed him back to his house in her car. Fortunately, there were no stranded vehicles on the side of the road to waylay them.

When he took her suitcase into a bedroom that looked unused, disappointment swamped her. He must want to convince her that he'd asked her there merely to protect her. Izzy guessed she would just have to change his mind.

The space was rather Spartan with a blue, ribbed bedspread, a nightstand with a lamp, and an old three-drawer dresser. No artwork hung on the wall, but a small, cluttered desk abutted one wall.

"Is this your office?"

"Yes, but don't worry. I won't disturb you."

That hadn't been her concern. She would be inconveniencing him. "Feel free to come in whenever you need." *Even if I'm in bed.*

He set down her case and walked her back to the living room. "Wine?" he asked.

If it would get him to loosen up, she'd have some. "Absolutely."

Izzy plopped down on the leather sofa and sank back against the cushions. Not knowing the exact time this spell had been cast, she couldn't know for sure when it would release. Just in case the effect wore off slowly, she held out her hand to create a swirl of wind around her body. Damn. She wasn't even able to make her blouse flutter.

"Any luck?" Rye asked, walking out of the kitchen.

He must have seen her hover her hand over her stomach. "No. I'll have to be patient."

He placed the two glasses on the coffee table in front of the sofa then sat next to her. "We'll get this guy, I promise."

"You'd think he'd figure out rather quickly that there are a lot of shifters in this town looking for him."

Rye picked up his glass, propped his feet up on the table and leaned close. "Not to scare you, but we've never learned much about the Changelings—who they are, how many there are, or even how they're organized. Your stalker could have his own team of Changelings watching out for him."

"Can't you sense who they are?"

"Not really. A regular werewolf gives off the same signature as a Changeling, but often my creep meter goes haywire if I get close to one. It doesn't help that not all *regular* shifters live in this compound."

Izzy sipped the delicious chilled wine, enjoying the musky scent and savoring the fruity tang as it slid down her throat, helping to take the edge off her nerves.

"How did my stalker know who to go to for help?"

Rye raised one shoulder. "There are several less than savory places in town where one might extract such information. If the Scotsman had money, he could learn a lot."

"You should pool your resources and hire a shifter from another town to infiltrate that group."

Rye laughed then tipped back his drink. "I love it. I'll be sure to suggest that sting operation to Kalan."

She didn't believe him, but that was okay. Right now, she just needed one Changeling to be found and taken down.

"Do they have any leads on the fire at Donaldson's warehouse?" she asked.

His chin tucked under and then he set his glass on the table. "How did you hear about that?"

"Not only is Teagan friends with Becky Donaldson, but it was on the news. Teagan said her dad had insurance on the building, but that it was still a financial hit to the family when the building was destroyed. Apparently, he was planning on fixing it up and selling it."

"That's a shame, but I'm not the arson investigator. I'm sure they'll find the person responsible." He didn't sound convinced.

"What if it was one of these Changelings?"

"Shouldn't make a difference. They're not invincible. They have jobs in town just like everyone else. It's only a matter of time before whoever is guilty is caught."

"All this talk about the stalker and his kind is making me depressed."

Rye lifted the glass from her fingers and set it down on the table next to his. "Oh, yeah? What would make you happy?"

Good. Her pity ploy had worked. With the way his eyes had lightened and his stubble had darkened, he wanted the same thing she did. "This."

In one quick move, Izzy straddled his lap. His eyes gleamed as his eyeteeth elongated. His inability to hide his interest was such a turn on. She wanted to block out all the bad crap that had occurred since that last fateful day in Scotland. The only good thing to come out of it was finding Ryerson McKinnon. He wasn't even her kind, yet they were definitely kindred souls. She could feel it. The tiny blue sparks randomly jumping off her skin proved it, though with the level of her excitement, she should be glowing blue. Damn, binding spell. When it did return, she hoped she didn't freak him out when she shimmered blue during wild, passionate sex—sex she planned to have very soon.

Planting her palms on the sides of his face, she leaned forward and kissed him hard. As if he'd sent out an electric pulse of his own, a current passed through her and ignited her from head to toe. Needing to taste more of him, she invited him inside. He slid his hands up her back and she threaded her fingers through his thick dark hair. The word *more* echoed in her head. Tongues tangling and breaths mingling, she reached down to unbutton her jeans with her right hand. Rye must have noticed, for he slid an arm under her butt and stood up with the two of them sealed together. He closed his eyes then opened them part way.

"I need more room," he said, breaking the kiss. "Stop me now, or hang on for one hell of a ride."

"Just so you know, if *you* stop this time, when I have my powers back, I'll be coming after you for payback."

He laughed as he carried her toward the bedroom. "There won't be any stopping this time, witchy woman. You're all mine."

Thrills shimmied across her skin as Rye nudged open the door to his room with his toe. The bed wasn't made and some of his clothes were tossed carelessly on a chair, but she didn't care. All she wanted was Rye, and she'd take him anyway she could have him.

He placed her on the bed, slipped off her sandals then stepped back. "Forgive me if I stop and start. I want you so much that my wolf will try to get out, and I can't let that happen."

While she'd never been in a position to have a lover shift on her—because she'd never made love to a *Were* before—she could see the hazards of that happening. "I understand."

He kicked off his shoes and unbuttoned his jeans.

Izzy sat up on the bed and nodded. "May I?"

Rye lowered his hand then rubbed his crotch as if he was willing it to deflate. "You're asking for trouble."

"I'll be careful." This time she hoped there'd be no unexpected visitors to interrupt them. "Move a little closer."

Enjoying Rye's dick while not tipping him over the climactic edge would be difficult, but she was determined to try. Remembering he was commando, she carefully lowered his jeans to his thighs, marveling at his size.

"Don't stare too long. I can only take so much before I weaken and possess you." Rye ground out each word as if he was using all of his restraint not to ravish her right away.

"I'm sorry, but I'm wondering if you'll fit. I've never been with someone as large as you."

"I'll be gentle and go slow—or at least I'll try."

Izzy had stalled long enough. The second she drew his cock toward her, he hissed, acting as if he was on the brink after one touch. Believing she had seconds rather than minutes, she drew him deep into her mouth and sucked hard.

"Izzy, geez, your mouth is like velvet and your tongue is causing electric sparks to ignite my dick."

While his comment was totally over-the-top, Rye sounded sincere, and she saw no reason to break the seal just to answer him.

With her free hand, she grabbed his nice hard ass and drew him closer. In response, he clutched a hunk of her hair and tugged. His woodsy scent and powerful muscles began to soothe her from the inside out. She flicked her tongue up and down his shaft while pumping and twisting her fist.

All of a sudden, he pulled out of her grasp. "Enough. If I don't take you right now, I'll lose it."

She loved how everything was exaggerated when it came to how much he wanted her. Just as she was about to ask what she could do to help, Rye stepped out of his jeans and practically tore his shirt off. With his gaze focused solely on her, he crossed his arms. "Take off your top."

Not that she had a problem doing it, but she was surprised he'd asked. "I thought you'd want to."

"The moment I touch you, I'll need to devour you."

Okay, then. The shirt it was. Izzy lifted it over her head and tossed it to the end of the bed. "Bra too?"

"Yes." His eyes were glowing a gorgeous yellow green, and she wanted to drink in his beauty.

Reaching behind her, she unhooked the clasp and slowly eased the straps down her shoulders, hoping he wouldn't be put off by her small breast size. His chest rose and fell in rapid succession. Once exposed, she placed the bra next to her.

"Let me have that," he commanded.

Izzy had the sense not to ask why. "Here…"

Rye closed his eyes, brought the cup to his face, and inhaled audibly. "I can't get enough of your scent. It's driving me wild."

"Then take me."

Without him asking, Izzy slipped off her pants, along with her black lacy panties. When she tossed them on top of her shirt, his gaze latched onto them, acting as if he was going to take those too, but instead, he returned his focus to her face. Like an animal after its prey, he crawled onto the bed and opened her legs wide.

"The wolf in me is growling and clawing to let him escape."

The moment Izzy opened her arms to welcome him, he pounced. As if his werewolf alter ego had released, he kissed her with so much passion, every cell in her body ignited.

He broke the kiss. "I love your blue halo. It means you want me, right?"

"You don't need to see the blue to know that." Not waiting for him to respond, she wrapped her arms around his back. When she dragged her fingers across his corded muscles, pure pleasure pulsed throughout her whole body.

As his hard cock pressed heavily against her stomach, their tongues jockeyed for position. Breaking the kiss, he slid downward and captured a nipple. For a second, she wondered if she had some kind of animal in her, since something was beating really hard inside her too.

One quick tug on her other breast, and dampness pooled between her thighs.

Beg him for more.

Izzy had never been this desperate. What was wrong with her? One kiss and one twist threatened to release her climax.

"Fuck," Rye said. "I forgot a condom."

"I'm on the pill. And I'm clean." She didn't want to wait any longer.

"I just got tested for my annual at the station."

"Good. Now hurry."

Rye switched his attention back to her first breast while he kneaded the second one. For someone who said he was desperate, he sure was taking his time. She lifted her hips to give him the hint.

As if he could read her mind, Rye slipped lower. One lick would go a long way to satisfying her. When he spread her folds and dipped two fingers into her wetness, she clutched the sheets for dear life.

His expert fingers twisting around and around almost made her come, but she wanted to prove to Rye that she was strong too. When he pressed on one spot in particular, she bucked and yelled. "You better fuck me now or forever hold your piece."

Heat raced up her face at the unexpected command. Izzy had never been the aggressor in bed, but with Rye it felt so right. Instead of impaling her, though, he licked her repeatedly. Crazy shifter. He had more control than she did. As he continued his sensual assault, flames engulfed her and she nabbed his shoulders and dug her nails into his skin. Her inner walls cramped with need. "Damn you, Ryerson."

"Hold on. It's about to get rougher, babe." Rye must have sensed she was close to exploding because he rose to his knees and flipped her over. He lifted her butt, forcing her onto her elbows. Placing his cock at her needy entrance, he palmed her tits and pressed them together.

Now he was just being cruel. Deciding it was time to take some control, Izzy pressed her hips back, but all that accomplished was to drive his cock in partway. Only then did she realize that he was just too damn big to fit.

Chapter Twelve

"**D**ON'T DO THAT again," Rye growled. "I'm trying not to shift."

If he hadn't taken so damned long, Izzy wouldn't have had to resort to pressing back on him. "Okay."

"I have to go slow."

That would test her resolve. True to his word, Rye seesawed in slowly until he was fully seated. Her inner walls were stretched to the max, but his fullness turned her on like never before. As he started to ease out, she tightened her hold on him. Having him inside her was wondrous, and she wanted to keep him there a bit longer.

He pinched her nipples and sharp pulses shot straight between her legs, forcing her to release the tension of her inner walls. If only she had her powers, she'd light a fire under him or send a blast of wind behind him. Izzy lowered her head to the bed and the angle of his cock shifted.

"Oh, fuck it." Rye palmed her breasts, withdrew, and then drove in hard.

Whoa. As pleasure consumed her, stars burst on the back of her lids. He planted his chest on her back and kissed her shoulder, almost as if he needed to distract himself.

"Yes, yes, yes," she moaned.

As if his inner beast truly had escaped, he pounded into her over and over again, pushing her way past her limits of control. Without warning, his sharp fangs dug into her neck, transporting her elsewhere. The lack of pain surprised her and shot her into another dimension where her climax swept her away.

Rye released his hold on her neck, and as his hot seed filled her, he let out something that sounded close to a howl. His hands tightened around her waist, and he licked the spot he'd bitten. Izzy never wanted to move again, but Rye eventually pulled out.

"Be right back." He trotted out of the bedroom and returned a few seconds later with a warm wet towel and cleaned her up. "Listen. I'm sorry. I didn't mean to bite you. I got too excited."

Izzy rolled over not sure how to respond. In truth, the bite had stimulated parts of her she hadn't known existed. Hell, maybe it would help get her powers back sooner. "It didn't hurt."

"No? I'm glad." He crawled in next to her and held her close. "You okay with sleeping here with me?"

She laughed. "I think it's a little late to be asking that."

"Perhaps. You're not the type to thrash about, are you?"

Izzy tapped his nose. "I'm sure you can handle me if I do."

"You got that right."

THE NEXT DAY was rather surreal. First, Izzy had woken up completely disoriented, not used to having a large man in her bed—or rather being in his bed. When she'd reflected on the amazing time they'd had the night before, she smiled. To her surprise, the fact he bit her didn't bother her, as it had been a result of being overly stimulated.

Rye had nudged her awake, and then went to fix her a great breakfast. She had to admit that staying at his place had been the best choice.

Even though Rye had to be at the station earlier than she needed to be at the spa, he insisted they drive in together. As long as she promised not to go into the back alley, he said she should be safe.

To her surprise, when he dropped her off, her mom was already at the store. Her mother stopped arranging the candles on the storefront window, and ran her gaze over Izzy from head to her toe. "There's something different about you this morning."

"You're changing the display?"

"I thought it needed a little sprucing up. Now don't change the subject."

The truth would come out sooner or later. Sometimes it sucked having a powerful mother who was way too intuitive. "Because that man tried to take me, Rye insisted I stay at his place. He said the Changeling's powers would be diminished if he even stepped foot inside their compound."

"I've never heard of that before."

"Me neither." Hmm. Perhaps Rye had told her that so she'd agree to stay with him. Regardless, it had been for the best.

"Did you sleep with him?"

Izzy froze, not sure how much to tell. "Geez Mom, I'm twenty-seven years old. That's none of your business."

"It most certainly is my business if he mated with you." She stepped closer, and Izzy slapped a hand over her slightly swollen puncture wound.

She couldn't tell if her mother was angry, concerned, or dare she say happy. "If you must know, he bit me in a moment of passion."

"Then he's mated to you." She lowered her chin. "You do know that in order to complete the mating, your blue orb needs to encompass both of you?"

"I know the facts of life." Jeez—at least the part about if she ended up with another Wendayan their glows needed to combine. She didn't know it applied to being with a *Were*. Now she knew.

Her mother moved even closer. "Let me see the marking on your back."

"Why?"

She placed her hands on Izzy's shoulders. "I can see I've failed you by not explaining what happens when you mate with a shifter, not that it happens often."

She thought it would never be an issue. "What do you mean?"

Her heart jumped to her throat.

Her mom twisted her around and lowered her shirt. "So it's true. Have you seen this?"

"Only my whole life," Izzy spun back around, a bit irritated at her mom's odd reaction.

"You now have a paw print underneath the vine. This means you two are mates for *life*—should you agree."

Her breath hitched. "Rye's hot, and I feel safe around him, but forever is a long time."

"Are you in love with him?" Suddenly, her mom's tone had lightened. "I realize that you played together growing up, but you hadn't seen him in years."

Why was she asking? "It's too early to tell."

Her mom huffed out a breath. "I'm glad you're being cautious. Our communities are quite tight, but cross-breeding has rarely occurred as far as I know. I never understood why not, but I always figured Naliana had her reasons. Just so you know, if you decide he's not the man for you, you can walk away and find another that suits you better. In time, that paw print will fade. Wendayans aren't bound if a shifter mates with them, but Rye is committed to you. He can only have one mate, and apparently, you're the one for him."

Izzy didn't know how to respond. "Not that I'm planning on it, but can't he mate again if I leave?"

"No. Shifters without their mate go crazy eventually or die."

"That's horrible."

"I didn't make the rules. I'll admit I'm a bit disappointed that he bit you without explaining the consequences, but he's the one who will suffer if you decide you don't want him." Mom held up a hand. "However, in my humble opinion, it's a real honor for a Wendayan to be with a shifter—especially a McKinnon."

Izzy stood straighter. "I think it's an equal honor that he's with a Berta. After all, we are a rather powerful family."

Mom smiled. "We are indeed."

Izzy tried to recall what Rye had said about mating—or if he'd said anything at all. She'd been so wrapped up with losing her powers that she might not have heard everything he'd said. "It was my fault that we ended up in bed. Look can we not discuss this anymore? I'm still trying to process everything."

"Sure, but you need to be thinking about whether you're ready to be an Alpha's wife. That's a big responsibility."

Izzy held up both hands. "Whoa. We had sex once! It's not like he asked me to marry him." Though after last night, the idea held a lot of appeal.

"Shifters—whether wolves, bears, or whatever—are a highly possessive breed. You could do worse, and the McKinnon blood is strong."

Izzy had to change the subject. Too much was being tossed at her at once. "Duly noted, now, where's my sister?" Usually she drove in with Mom, though the shop wouldn't be opening for a little while.

"Missy has the day off, and I told Teagan she could rest too."

Mom always liked to have three of them at the store in town in case she needed to work on a McKinnon or a Murdoch at Izzy's house. Given both the Alpha and the Beta were on a cruise, she probably wouldn't be needed. "May I ask why?"

Her mother glanced to the front door. "Dad and I think it would be best if you kept busy. Having four of us here won't allow that. But being here doesn't include you visiting your father every few hours. He can take care of himself."

Izzy planted a hand on her hip. "Are you worried that creep will come after me again?"

"Honestly? Yes. Until your powers return, we want you safe."

As much as Izzy wanted to argue, she had to agree with her for now. She was rather helpless against him. "What do you want me to do first?"

"You can clean the back room for starters. Mrs. Farrell will be in shortly."

Not having the energy to argue, Izzy headed to the rear of the store. No sooner had she cleaned that room than her mom gave her another chore. By lunchtime, she was giving serious thought to looking for a teaching job. To make matters worse, her father came over with sandwiches from the deli, saying he didn't want her going out to eat alone. Sheesh. Here she thought Rye was overprotective. These two were worse.

For the rest of the day, she performed some aura cleansings, gave massages, or played cashier. With only the two of them there, she was indeed busy.

A few minutes before closing, Rye arrived to drive her back to his place, and unexpected joy filled her. Compared to her folks, he was pure freedom.

As much as she wanted to pummel him with questions about this mating stuff, doing so might imply she'd accepted that they were going to be together permanently. For her own sanity, she wanted to wait a little bit longer before she decided.

Rye spoke with her mom then escorted her out. "How was your day?" he asked.

"Busy." As he led her to his truck, she glanced around. "I trust you-know-who isn't near."

He shook his head. "I wouldn't have let you out of the building if he had been."

That was one benefit of being with a shifter. He could detect when another one was near. "So are you going to lock me in your house for the night?"

He opened the truck door and looked around as she crawled in. "I might if you don't behave." Rye grinned. "But first, I thought you might like to go to your special spot and test your powers."

"Yes!" That was so sweet of him. "I've been chomping at the bit to try something, but I didn't dare do anything inside the store. It would be horrible if I ended up setting the place on fire."

Rye looked over at her and raised his brows. "Speaking of which, I'd feel more comfortable if you stuck to making waves on the lake or growing a plant. We don't need a forest fire."

"I promise. Fire's my weakest talent anyway. Dad is the amazing one. His accuracy is something I aspire to someday. My aim sucks—kind of like my pool game."

Rye laughed then started the engine. "I'll be sure not to piss you off."

She hoped he was kidding. "You should know that I only use my talents under dire circumstances."

"Like when you ensnared that Changeling?"

"Exactly."

Once they turned into Wendaya Cove, Rye drove past her house toward the small lake. He parked and helped her out then withdrew a basket from the truck bed. "Thought we'd have a picnic."

She looped an arm through his. "You are amazing, though we could have gone out to dinner. With you at my side, surely my stalker won't try anything."

"You're assuming he'd come alone. Though I'm confident I could best one of them, if three attacked me all at once, I'm not so sure I'd be victorious."

Shivers traipsed up her body. "All the more reason to pray my powers will return soon."

Rye nodded, though his pinched brows implied he didn't want to rely on a woman to save him. "Where would be a good place to set up? I want to watch you do some magic," he asked.

"I know a good spot."

On the other side of the rock outcrop was a small pine tree area, lined with pine needles that was far enough from the water so that any wind tunnel she created on the lake wouldn't affect him, but close enough so that he'd have a good view.

She led him over to her choice spot. "How about here?"

"Perfect."

From inside the basket, he retrieved a small blanket that he spread out. "How about I finish setting up while you see if your powers have returned?" he said.

"That would be great. I won't be long." Izzy wanted to give him a thank you kiss, but if she did, she feared they wouldn't be able to stop. Creating a waterspout was something she'd been able to do since she was young, so she decided to start with that simple task.

Stepping to the edge of the water she inhaled, hoping that the witch's curse had worn off. Pretending she was stirring the water with an invisible spoon, a small spout formed and her heart hammered. She then lifted her arm to increase its size. Wanting to add a bit of wind to the mix, she blew out a breath. Instead of the large spout she desired, the cone of water rose two feet then fell. Well, crap. She tried a few more times but had the same results.

Izzy glanced back at Rye who thankfully didn't seem to be paying attention to her failures. If she couldn't manage wind or water, perhaps she'd attempt to grow something. Izzy found a patch of ferns and lowered her hand over the area. With a twirl of her fingers, one plant lifted its fronds and grew. Pulse beating fast, she willed it to reach her hand. Unfortunately, it stopped after two more feet. Her shoulders sagged, but it was better than yesterday's attempts.

Content with the small progress, she worked her way back up to Rye.

"How did it go?" he asked.

"It wasn't a total loss." She explained the extent of her abilities.

"You should be good as new tomorrow."

"I hope so." She sat cross-legged and picked up one of the sandwiches he'd purchased. "Can we talk about that bite you gave me?"

Rye glanced to the side. "I'm sorry. I should have asked you first, but shit, when I'm with you, my need is out of control."

"It's all good. My mom noticed the bite and said we were mated. Was that your intention?"

He blew out a breath, appearing out of sorts. "Intention? I don't know, but what I do know is that you are my mate."

Her temple throbbed. "How did you know?"

"Your scent drives me crazy, the wolf in me wants to protect you to the death, and be with you forever."

"What about Rye, the man?"

He stroked her face. "He wants all of that too."

She leaned back on her elbows to study him. "Why did you think I'd be okay with it? After all, we are different breeds."

The corner of his lip curled up. "The blue aura around you when we were in the front seat of your car was my first clue. That and how you seemed to enjoy poking that pool cue at my crotch."

She laughed, loving the release in tension. Izzy couldn't deny the sexual attraction. Izzy turned her back to Rye and tugged down her T-shirt. "Do you see the paw print that appeared on my shoulder?"

He finger traced the spot. "It's beautiful." When she twisted around, Rye had his shirt off. "Has mine changed?"

"No."

He turned back around. "I thought not. I've been told that when you accept the mating it will change."

"How did my change? I mean it wasn't like you secretly inked me."

"I don't know. It just did." Rye moved closer and picked up her hands. "So now you know. We are mates."

"What happens next? Will I suddenly shift into a wolf or something?" Two of her human friends had been mated to a bear shifter and they'd learned to transform between species.

"I don't even know if a Wendayan has ever mated with a shifter before, so I can't say for sure." This time, it was Rye who leaned back on his elbows, and he looked highly appealing. Something about him today appeared stronger and more virile.

"My mom said she thought one had a long time ago."

He sat up. "Really, do you know who it was?"

"No. Mom didn't know either, but why should it matter?"

"I'd hate to have you try to shift, only to have your own powers diminished."

Her pulse quickened at the horrible thought. "You think that would happen?"

"I really have no idea, but I think we should be cautious. I know how important your magic is to you." He leaned toward her.

Having Rye a few inches closer made her heartbeat soar. "You are a sweet man."

Actually, he was a lot more than just sweet. Perhaps the partial return of her powers was doing a number on her head. Then again, all during work, she couldn't keep her thoughts off Rye. Her body kept cramping with need.

While she'd never heard of a Wendayan mating call, thanks to a mom who wasn't the most forthcoming when it came to *the* sex talk, Izzy believed she was experiencing one now.

"If you want to try to learn to shift, I'm game to teach you, but we have to wait until the white moon appears. That's the first time a human who has been bitten by a shifter would be able to shift."

Now that she had asked, she questioned her desire. "I'll think about it. In truth, sometimes it's hard enough to refrain from using my magical powers. Can you imagine if I could shift too?"

"You'd be one freaking powerhouse, but if you had to choose between the two, which would you pick?" He held up a hand. "Not that you really have a choice, but I figure if you don't even *try* to shift, the gods might let you keep your powers."

Goose bumps raced up her flesh. "I never want to be without my magic. I'd gladly leave shifting to you."

"On the other hand, you might be able to keep both."

"That's true too. I wish I could summon Naliana and ask her."

"Good luck with that." Rye nodded to her sandwich. "Don't you want to eat? You told me that you liked roast beef."

"I do." Here she'd chosen that sandwich and hadn't even sampled it. Rye distracted her in so many ways. Izzy took a big bite, and the spicy mustard with the medium-rare meat made her taste buds explode. "It's delicious. Thank you."

"My pleasure. It's possible you've received other benefits regardless of whether you have the ability to shift."

"Such as?" she asked, trying not to talk with her mouth full.

"You should be able to heal quickly."

She recalled how he'd been stabbed one day and was almost back to normal the next. How much of it was because of Missy's healing ways or his ability to shift, Izzy didn't know. "That would be nice, but let's not test your theory just yet." He chuckled. "Any other super powers you possess I should know about?"

"They're hardly super powers, but you should live a longer life because the lifespan of a shifter is considerably longer than it is for a human." He held up a hand. "And a shifter will look younger longer too."

"I'd like that—especially the looking younger part."

He smiled. "Your skin is already like alabaster. If you take after your mother, you'll be fantastic at any age."

She set her sandwich down. "Thank you. Not that healing and living longer aren't already great bonuses, but is that all? I want to be prepared."

"You might be faster and stronger, but only time will tell."

Time. It was something she didn't have a lot of, especially when it came to deciding her fate. Rye moved closer, and she saw no reason not to kiss him. The moment their lips touched, it was as if Rye had suddenly possessed the power of creating fire, because her insides burned for him. Her level of need had escalated since yesterday, and as their tongues battled for position, she straddled him, not able to get close enough.

Rye slid his hands under her shirt and unhooked her bra. He then leaned back, breaking their kiss. "I needed this. You don't know how hard it was to be at the station and focus on work. I can't stop thinking about you."

That did it. It might not be smart to give into her lustful urges the day after their marathon lovemaking session, but since he'd bitten her, it seemed her need had grown by leaps and bounds. Whether it was a result of her powers being out of whack, or something Rye had done, she didn't know. "I need you too."

"Give me some room." Rye scooted out from under her and toed off his shoes. "You don't think that witch lady will be back, do you?"

She glanced around. "Ophelia? I doubt it. Besides, it's rather secluded here." It was why she'd chosen it. As Rye's fingers latched onto his pants, she swatted them away. "Let me."

"Not on your life. One touch and I'll spontaneously combust. I don't want you to think that I only want you for sex, but damn, I can't keep from ravishing you."

She laughed, partly out of embarrassment. She'd been thinking the same thing. "Not at all. I figure since this is new, the only way to get this intense longing out of our systems is to seek release."

He grinned. "I love the way you think."

In a flash, Rye ditched the rest of his clothes. The sight took her breath away. "If I didn't need you so bad, I'd just drink you in," she said.

"You can do all the drinking you want afterward. Right now, I need to get you out of that rather prim and proper outfit."

Izzy glanced down at her what she was wearing. "There's nothing wrong with my white shirt."

"Unless you're naked, you're too prim for me."

She laughed, loving how this man could make her feel so special. "I say go for it."

Chapter Thirteen

HAVING RYE'S HANDS all over her would ratchet her desire, and she hoped her glow didn't go crazy and encompass him. If it did, it would be her total acceptance of being mated, and she needed a little more time.

When he undid the top button on her shirt, Izzy reached out and grabbed his hard shaft.

His eyes turned a golden green. "If you don't want me to rip this off of you, you better let go." He nearly growled his command, sounding like he was holding on by a thread.

Izzy released him. Watching him fumble with the tiny buttons on her blouse made her push his hands away. "Let me. Your paws are too big."

He held them up. "I am not a wolf yet."

Teasing him was fun. "Well, let's see if I can turn you into one."

Rye groaned and slipped off her shoes then managed to remove her pants and panties before she could take off her shirt and bra. Despite it being summer, there was a slight chill coming off the water and her nipples hardened.

"I see you need warming up," he said.

The next thing she knew, she was flat on her back and Rye was drawing a taut nipple into his mouth. The intensity of his touch was like nothing she'd ever experienced before, and she wondered if it was the bite that had altered something inside her.

Digging her nails into his shoulder, she arched her back, needing his cock. "Yes."

"I can't wait," he groaned.

Thank goddess. Lips locked, Rye drove into her and held still as if any movement would set him off. Izzy was sore from making love yesterday, and her inner walls were barely able to stretch enough to accommodate him, but she wouldn't stop for anything. She wrapped her legs around his waist and lifted her hips higher. Never breaking the kiss, their connection was so complete that she believed they were merging into one. He slid out a half-inch and she clamped down hard on him.

"Don't," he pleaded. When he closed his eyes, the hair grew on his face and his claws extended.

The next thrust went in so deep every nerve ignited, and Izzy lost the will to hold on any longer. She lowered her legs and planted her feet flat. On the brink of coming, she dropped her hips then lifted them quickly, causing his cock to drive deeper into her, sending her skyward. As his hot seed filled her, he howled and she yelled. Together they came so hard, the blood drained from her brain.

Gulping in air, every muscle gave way and the back of her knees met the ground. Words couldn't form. Rain clouds gathered overhead, but at the moment, she didn't care if she got drenched. Rye gathered her in his arms and rolled over so that she was now on top.

"We didn't last very long, did we?" she said.

He tapped her nose. "No. I've heard it will be like this for a while."

"Goddess in Heaven help us."

"Amen." Rye squeezed her butt. "For the record, I love when you glow."

"You cause me do it."

He grinned. "Let's get dressed so we can finish eating. We don't need to be caught in a storm."

He'd feel hurt if she tossed the food, though by now the ants and bugs might have attacked it. "Are you asking me to actually sit up?

None of my muscles seem to be working very well."

"No." With that, he slid her off of him and sat up. "I just thought you might be hungry."

She sat up. "Actually, you filled me up so much I'm good."

Rye laughed and Izzy sighed. Life with this man just might work out.

IZZY AND RYE spent the evening at his house playing silly card games and laughing. It was when he brought the chess set out that she called a halt to game day. "It's bad enough you beat me at pool, I don't need to be humiliated at chess."

"I can teach you," he said with a twinkle in his eye.

"I say we watch a movie and snuggle."

He grinned. "I'll let you have your way tonight, but only because I took advantage of you today."

Izzy wasn't going to give him the satisfaction of knowing that if he hadn't asked to take off her clothes, she would have stripped him naked.

No surprise, Rye let her pick the movie. She chose a romantic comedy, and the poor soul fell asleep halfway through. He looked so cute with his head on her shoulder, snoring away that she didn't have the heart to wake him since he had to rise earlier than usual tomorrow.

Due to his change in schedule, he agreed to let her drive her own car to work tomorrow. While they were fairly convinced her powers would be at full strength by morning, she had to promise to park in front of the spa instead of on the side near the alley.

Around eleven, she was ready for bed. As much as she wanted to cuddle with him, she let Rye snooze on the sofa. She even set his phone on the coffee table so he'd hear his alarm.

By the time she rose the next morning, Rye already had left for work. A note on the table said how much he enjoyed their night together, and she had to chuckle. Ten bucks said he had no idea the name of the movie they'd watched.

After changing into her a blue button-down shirt and jeans, Izzy headed into work, arriving in town without incident. She was beginning to wonder if that terrible man had finally realized it was best if he headed back to Scotland, since his window of opportunity had closed. Those forty-eight hours without her powers had been the scariest in her life.

With a bounce to her step, she entered the Crystal Winds Spa.

"You look happy," her mom said.

"I am." What Mom had said was true. Izzy should count her blessings that she had the chance to be mated to a McKinnon. After her talk with Rye about what that would entail, she was even more thrilled. Soon, she'd complete their mating ritual.

She'd called her mom last night to give them the good news that her powers were nearly at full strength. That might have been a slight exaggeration, but her parents' over protectiveness was wearing on her nerves.

"Did you learn any more from Rye?"

She probably meant about the mating. "I did, though Rye's not sure whether my powers will be affected or not, or if I'm even able to shift. To be honest, I don't want to take a chance on losing what I have."

Her mom rubbed her shoulder. "I'm proud of you."

Izzy hugged her quickly. "Thanks, Mom. That means so much to me."

Last night, while in bed, Izzy tried to picture what it might be like if the two of them could romp in the woods together. That image faded when she remembered her own ability to perform magic might be lost. She just hoped Rye wouldn't be disappointed if she decided not to be a shifter or if the gods willed it so. He'd have to be content to enjoy her wind swirling, water parting ways.

Unless… She spun to face her mom. "Do you think it's possible that when Rye bit me he could have received some of my Wendayan traits? It seems only fair."

Her brows furrowed. "I have no idea, but there's only one way to find out."

It would be so much fun to see if he could manipulate the elements. "I guess we'll have to see what he can do!"

With that thought, Izzy remained invigorated for the rest of the morning. As lunch drew near, she decided to see if Elana wanted to join her—safety in numbers so to speak. They had so much to catch up on.

"I'm going across the street to see if Elana is free for lunch," Izzy said.

Her mother finished making an entry into the computer and looked up. "Be careful."

"I will."

Earlier this morning, during a lull, she'd slipped into one of the back rooms. To her delight, Izzy had been able to force the air to lift a pile of sheets and send them swirling. Of course, it meant she had to pick them up afterward and fold them, but it had been worth it to prove she was at full strength once more.

Before Izzy stepped into the Blooms of Hope florist shop, she stopped to admire the display in the storefront window. A vase with three red roses and some baby's breath was prominently displayed. Attached was a helium balloon with a birthday message, and in front was a cute bear holding a heart. Aw, that was so sweet. Next to the bear was another display of wildflowers in a lime green vase next to a stuffed wolf. For some reason, her thoughts shot to children and she wondered what their kids might be like—though that was a long way off. Would they be magical and a *Were*, or just magical, or just a *Were*? She sighed.

Elana opened the front door and smiled, "You going to stare at the display or come inside?"

"Whoops. You did such a great job with this. Maybe you can give mom some pointers."

Elana laughed. "If she wants any." Elana held the door open and Izzy passed through. "I didn't expect to see you today."

"I wanted to see if you'd be up for lunch." The cooler on the right side of the store was jammed with colorful flowers, and several uncut ones sat on the counter.

"I'd love to. I take it your jailers are letting you out?"

Elana was well aware of how protective her parents had become. Izzy glanced around to make sure Elana's assistant wasn't close by. "My powers are back, so I'm able to leave, but only in the company of others," she whispered.

Elana did a fist pump. "Yes. I want to hear everything that's been going on. I live vicariously through your wonderful adventures."

"Well, having a stalker isn't exactly a good adventure."

Her friend glanced at the ceiling. "It is when someone as hot as Rye McKinnon comes to your rescue."

"True."

Just as Elana put away the rest of the flowers, Izzy's cell rang, but she didn't recognize the number. "Hello?"

"Izzy, this is Kalan Murdoch."

Her heart jumped a notch by the concern in his voice. "What's wrong?"

"It's Rye. He was inside a building putting out a fire when it partially collapsed." She grabbed onto the counter for support. Werewolves healed quickly she reminded herself. "Is he okay?"

"He's been taken to the hospital. I'm on my way there. I thought you should know."

"Thank you," she said, the two words sticking in her throat. As soon as Kalan disconnected, tears brimmed on her lashes. Her emotional calm had totally evaporated.

Elana grabbed her arm. "What is it?"

Izzy slowly faced her best friend. "Rye was in a burning building that collapsed."

"Oh my God, how is he?"

Her brain fogged. "I don't think Kalan said, other than Rye's at the hospital. I need to go to him."

"Then I'm driving. You're in no condition to navigate."

Elana was right. Normally, Izzy was cool under adverse conditions, but right now she was falling apart. "Okay."

Elana told her assistant she might be gone for the rest of the day, but she'd call with an update. Izzy and Elana darted outside. Thinking about Rye, Izzy didn't even look around. If her stalker had been out back, he might have been able to capture her without a fight since she wasn't sure she could even focus enough to use her powers.

"You should call your mom to let her know," Elana said once they were in the car.

Oh, crap. "You're right. I can see it now. If I didn't come back from lunch, Mom would call every shifter in town to search for me."

The phone call was short because Izzy didn't know much. Thankfully, her mother was supportive, telling her to take as much time as she needed.

By the time Elana pulled into the hospital parking lot, Izzy was a jittery mess. Her friend parked and together they entered the Emergency Room.

"You might not be able to see him right away, you know," Elana said. "You'll have to be patient."

"Patient my ass. I might be able to help."

Elana grabbed her arm. "Doing what? He doesn't need any more fire. Unless he's burning up and you can provide a cool breeze, you need to let the doctors do their job."

Rationally, Izzy understood that to be true, but emotionally, she wanted to help him anyway she could. She sucked at waiting though. Izzy rushed up to the nurses' station and asked about Rye with Elana right behind her. "He's a fireman and was brought in a little while ago."

As the nurse typed in the information, Kalan stepped out of one of the curtained rooms and strode toward her. "Izzy, hi." He glanced over at Elana and stilled.

Oh, no. It was bad. Izzy placed a hand on his shoulder. "Tell me. How is he?"

"He's going to be okay. He's in room 4 if you want to see him."

She spun around to Elana whose smiled had faltered. "Don't worry. I'll wait in the lounge."

Izzy was about to ask Kalan if he could look after her friend, but that would have been dumb. Nothing would happen to Elana in a hospital. Her thoughts in a scrambled mess, she rushed into Rye's room and halted at his prone form, an oxygen mask over his face. He must have sensed her for he opened his eyes, removed the mask, and smiled.

"Hey. You didn't need to come here."

Was he crazy? "Kalan called and said you'd been trapped in a burning building."

He pushed back on his elbows and patted the bed. "Have a seat."

Being so close to Rye would mess with her head, but she needed to make sure he was okay. "Put the mask back on."

Rye clasped her hand. "I'm fine. No burns either. The paramedics overreacted. Even if I had told them I wasn't suffering from smoke inhalation, they never would have believed me. This mask is precautionary. Besides, I didn't need to be advertising that I have some powers of my own."

Hearing Rye so calm helped settle her down. She rubbed his arm to give him assurance and suddenly hair sprouted. "Seriously?" she whispered. "What are you thinking about?"

His cheeks dimpled. "What I'm always thinking about—you."

She swatted at him. "You have to concentrate on healing."

He rubbed her leg. "Sex is what will help me heal the most."

She chuckled. "You're incorrigible."

"That's why you like me."

It was one of the reasons. "Get better first. Then we'll see."

He clasped her hand and sobered. "You know you didn't have to come all the way out here. You could have just asked me how I was."

He wasn't making any sense. "What do you mean?"

His mouth opened then closed. He then stared at her as if she was supposed to figure it out.

"You could have asked with your mind." That thought just floated into her head. It was almost as if Naliana had spoken to her, only it was Rye's voice even though his lips weren't moving.

She looked around as if someone had spoken then returned her gaze back to a smiling Rye. "I swore I heard your voice in my head."

"In my haste to discuss what it meant to be mated to a shifter, I totally forgot about our ability for mental telepathy. It doesn't matter that you haven't given your complete consent."

She would. Later. Her pulse soared. "Are you kidding? I mean Naliana and I—"

"It's just like that."

She had so many questions. "Can every shifter communicate this way?"

He laughed. "Only mates can." He held up a hand. "I take that back. Kalan and I can because I'm soon to be the Alpha and he's my Beta. Prior to a few weeks ago, we didn't have that link. My dad said that under extreme circumstances, once I'm Alpha, I'll be able to send out a message to our collective clan."

"I didn't know that about *Weres*. Have I had my head in the sand all this time?" Izzy must have been focused on perfecting her talents too much to notice. "Are my parents aware you can do this?"

He shrugged. "You'll have to ask them. As for you communicating with me, you just have to picture us together and direct your thoughts."

That seemed easy enough. Izzy closed her eyes and remembered being on her back on the blanket by the lake, and the memory of intense pleasure filled her. *"I want you,"* she telepathed.

"I want you too," he said out loud.

Izzy opened her eyes. "Oh, my goddess, it worked!"

"It did. See how cool it is to be my mate?"

She didn't have the chance to respond because the doctor strode in, and Izzy jumped off the bed to give him room. Thankfully, he didn't ask her to leave. After he checked out Rye's breathing, he scribbled something on a pad.

"You're lucky. The smoke inhalation could have been worse. Next time, get out in time," the doctor said.

"Yes sir."

"I'm signing your release papers, but I want you to rest for the remainder of the day."

Rye glanced over at her and smiled. "No problem."

As much as she wanted a repeat performance of their experience by the lake, she'd make certain he remained still.

"Do you have a ride home?" the doctor asked.

She piped up. "A friend drove me here, but I'm sure she can give him a lift."

"*Thank you,*" Rye telepathed, and she received it loud and clear. "*Kalan said he couldn't stay,*" he told her.

That was interesting. Betas were supposed to have their Alphas' back. Once the doctor left, Rye needed to change out of his hospital gown, and if she watched him undress, she might do something stupid. "I'll wait for you in the visitor's lounge."

"Afraid you'll be tempted?"

He could not read her mind. Could he? She grinned. "I'd love nothing better than to look at your hot ass through the opening of that sexy gown, but we need to get you home."

Izzy found Elana and assured her that Rye would be fine. "I hope you don't mind, but I kind of volunteered you to drive him back to the shop."

"Certainly." She ran a comforting hand down Izzy's arm.

With that worry gone, she turned her concern to Rye's friend. "Did you speak with Kalan when I was in with Rye?"

"He told me a little about what happened then ran off."

"Did Kalan say why he had to leave? Rye seemed a bit perplexed why he hadn't stayed."

Elana shrugged. "No." She huffed out a laugh. "Poor man must have been quite upset because he ran into the door."

Izzy laughed—not at Kalan, but at the relief that ran through her. "I totally understand. You saw how I was a total basket case."

Elana smiled. "You really care for him, don't you?"

There was no denying that she was going to mate with Ryerson McKinnon. "Yes, I do."

Chapter Fourteen

"**S**IT," IZZY COMMANDED. "You heard the doctor." Sheesh, Rye was more stubborn than anyone in her family.

"I'm fine." He dropped down onto the sofa, propped his feet up on the coffee table, and crossed his arms.

She didn't believe for a moment that he'd stay there. "I'm about to cook an early dinner, and I don't need you rubbing your body against mine and distracting me."

"Suit yourself," he said. *"However, that won't stop me from mentally tormenting you. I'll tell you how I plan to lick your pussy and then drive my cock so deep into you that—"*

"Stop!" Izzy laughed. The man had a one-track mind. "I'm making a chicken casserole, so if you don't want it tough, stay put and keep out of my head."

"You can't keep a good man down for long."

She shook her head.

Even with trying to keep from worrying about him, it took several minutes to find all the pots and pans in his kitchen. Izzy had already itemized what he had in the refrigerator and pantry, so her choices of what to make had been limited. If he planned to ask her to stay with him for any length of time, there'd have to be a shopping trip in their near future.

"Find everything?" he asked, humor lacing his voice.

"Don't you worry about a thing. I'll ask if I need help." It was difficult enough not to walk across the dining room and have her way with him. Ever since he'd bitten her, her sexual urges had grown exponentially. If she wasn't careful, those desires might inhibit her ability to do her magic.

She dumped the chicken in the dish then read the directions on the back of the box.

"Mind if I watch TV?" he asked.

Bring two cups of water to a boil and then add the rice. "Go right ahead."

"Whoa. Add head? Sure. You can give me head anytime. Come and get it."

She laughed. "Whoops. I see I might need a bit of practice with this telepathy thing. I meant to say to go right ahead."

Rye smiled and turned on the tube. Most likely he'd twisted her words on purpose. She cleaned the kitchen then organized his dishes while the chicken cooked. Once it finished, she served the meal and was delighted Rye's appetite seemed to be as good as new. Perhaps his body had already healed from the smoke inhalation.

He patted his stomach. "I could get used to this," he said. "Where did you learn to cook so well?"

"My mom taught me growing up, but I also took advantage of some cooking classes in Italy and France."

"Well, you can cook for me anytime."

She smiled, but Izzy wasn't quite sure what he meant. If she was his mate, she assumed she'd be staying with him. Right? So many of the rules confused her.

After dinner, Rye stood and when he gathered some of the plates, she held up her hand. "I'll clean up. You sit."

He ignored her and placed the dishes in the sink. "Believe me, I'd be the first to take it easy if I wasn't back to normal. How about we go outside and I'll demonstrate my strength for you."

She wasn't sure that was a good idea, but even if she insisted he take it easy, he wouldn't agree. "I like the outside part, but you don't have to prove anything to me." She wanted to step closer but knowing her, one kiss would lead to more heated things.

Rye held out a hand. "Let's go then."

She was game. The fresh air always invigorated her. "Where to?"

"To Silver Lake."

She sighed, remembering the days when she used to play there. Sunshine and swimming filled her with sweet memories. "I haven't been there since I was a little kid."

"I'm curious to know if you think it has changed." Rye wrapped an arm around her waist and led her down the path that followed the roadway. "I love it here. I can't imagine ever leaving."

"There's no place like home, and I speak from experience." She'd been hesitant at first to leave her idyllic life style in Europe, but once she was home again, she could see what she'd been missing.

He smiled. "I'm glad. You mentioned you might apply for a teaching job for the fall. How's that coming?"

"I haven't applied yet, but I probably will soon. As much as I love working at the Crystal Winds Spa, it might be nice to branch out. Don't get me wrong. I love my mom, but always being around my whole family can sometimes be a bit—"

"Overwhelming and claustrophobic?"

She chuckled, "Yes to both of those."

"I get it. Try being the next in line to be Alpha. Talk about responsibility. Dad is always lecturing me about how to do this and how to do that. When my parents return from their vacation and he passes the honor onto me, I'm going to work hard to do things my own way."

She liked that he wanted to take charge. "Do you sometimes wish you hadn't been born first?"

"When I was young, I used to think that, but as I got older, I realized that I relish being the leader. I enjoy being a fireman too, but I want the best for our Clan." His grip on her waist tightened. "Let's cut through at the next turn off."

Right before the road split, someone came toward them from the opposite direction. "That's Chelsea!" she said.

"With Badger."

They met up and Chelsea hugged her brother. "I ran into Kalan in town, and he said you were in the hospital. Why didn't you call me?" She ran her gaze up and down his body.

"I didn't want to worry anyone. I was fine. The smoke didn't affect me." He explained how the building had collapsed as he was putting out the fire. "Do me a favor. When the folks return, please don't mention it? I don't want to upset Mom."

Izzy bent down to play with the puppy. He was so cute.

"Actually, I was on my way to see you. Mom and Dad just returned from their cruise."

Rye looked off to the side, acting as if he was trying to remember when they were supposed to be home. "Did they have a good time?"

"An amazing one, but be careful about asking or you'll have to sit through the slide show of all of Dad's badly exposed pictures. I think there are more photos of Mom than there are of the scenery."

He chuckled. "We'll be sure to stop by."

Chelsea smiled. "They're having a party tomorrow night, and both of you are invited."

"Not that I mind, but did you tell them about us?" he asked.

"Not me. I didn't think it was my place to break the news, but Finn told me he saw you two at the bar and that Molly waited on you. If they invited Izzy, they must know you two are together."

"Can't keep anything secret around here, can I?" he said.

Izzy laughed and stood. "I keep forgetting what a small town we live in. I'd love to see your folks again. What can I bring?" she asked Chelsea.

"Perhaps a dessert?"

Izzy was happy she wouldn't have to come empty-handed. "You got it."

They discussed time and logistics. "I have tomorrow off, so that won't be an issue," Rye said. "We'll be there."

The two of them hugged, and Chelsea went on her way. As nice as it was to see his sister, Izzy wanted to spend some alone time with Rye. When they weren't clawing at each other to take off their clothes, they found interesting things to talk about.

As they emerged from the tree-lined path, the shimmering lake spread out before them. Rays from the early evening sun bounced off the surface, making the entire area magical. "It's beautiful," she said.

"The lake inspires me. There's a spot where I like to sit and reflect. Wanna see?" Rye had suddenly grown quiet, and his more serious side intrigued her as well.

"Absolutely." She'd loved to learn more about him.

They were partway around the lake when a tall figure emerged from the trees. It was James.

"Hello there," James said.

Izzy still couldn't believe he would live forever. As much as she loved life, she wasn't sure she wanted to if everyone she cared for was long gone, though James at least had Naliana, though it was only once a month.

"James." Rye shook hands with the man.

James studied her. "Have any luck with the return of your powers?"

It wasn't so much that she wanted to show off, as it was to confirm she was at full strength. Izzy turned around and swept up the air in front of her, focusing on the water itself. With a twist of her hand, the water rose, twirled, and then skipped across the surface.

James clapped. "That's amazing."

Izzy let the water drop. "Thanks. I guess I'm back to normal."

Rye drew her close as if to present a unified front. "Any news about Izzy's stalker yet?"

James nodded. "Some. If my source is correct, the man's name is Owen Chancellor and he's from Scotland. Supposedly, he wants to take Izzy back to his home. For what purpose, my source didn't know."

Dread collided with relief at being able to put a name to the face.

"Do you know where he is now?" Rye asked, the grip on her waist tightening.

"No," James said, "but I've asked my source to dig deeper."

With that, James turned and disappeared into the woods. Izzy squinted to catch a glimpse of the fleeting figure, but the man was truly gone. "Is he capable of disappearing? One minute he was heading down the trail and the next he wasn't there."

"I have no idea. I wouldn't put anything past the gods though. Naliana has asked for favors before—like saving James from certain death. For all we know, she asked for the cloak of invisibility too."

"Now that's a trait I'd like," she said.

Rye leaned over and kissed her forehead. "You have enough powers, my witchy woman. Anymore and I'll get an inferiority complex."

From the glint in his eyes, he was only kidding, but it did remind her that he might have some of her traits. "If you could perform some of my magic, what would you like it to be?"

His brows rose. "I think everything you do is way cool, though as a kid I used to pretend I was a dragon."

She laughed. "Did you want to fly?"

"Not really. Mostly I just wanted to shoot fire at things."

Izzy scrunched up her nose at the image of this adorable little boy setting things ablaze. "Like what?"

His cheeks dimpled. "Anything that would burn."

"That's such a guy thing." And she loved him for it. There would come a time when she'd explain to him how to test for his possibly acquired new talents.

They continued to walk around the lake until he stopped and motioned toward a large rock. "I used to sit here for hours, daydreaming. Come on."

Rye helped her up then sat next to her. "What did you dream about?" she asked.

"A little bit of everything, but mostly what it would be like to stay in my wolf form forever."

It seemed likely that she would never experience that. "What did you imagine it would it be like?"

"For starters, I'd be surrounded by friends while I roamed wherever I wanted. Basically, I could just enjoy the outdoors. I wouldn't have to work or have many responsibilities." He lowered his gaze. "Just so you know, I was ten at the time. You?"

Her life had been so different and not nearly as fun. "I wasn't much of a dreamer. From the time I was little, it was drilled into me how different I was. Having the ability to control the elements was and still is a big responsibility. I wasn't given a lot of chances to just be myself."

"I'm sorry. I can't imagine not running free. It's part of who I am."

What she wouldn't give to run free like that. "My life wasn't all bad. I did have my magic."

"True, but not being able to share it with others must have been hard."

She looked deep into his eyes. He understood, and that meant the world to her. "It was, but that's the fate of most Wendayans."

"Most?"

"Society seems to accept those like my sister who have the power to heal, and those who are psychics, as they've been around for years, but my talents are a lot less mainstream."

Rye leaned back on his elbows, a gleam in his eye. "Want to have some fun now?"

She laughed. "What kind of fun? I can't shift, remember?"

"Not yet. You'll have to wait until the white moon."

Is that what he wanted? From the excitement in his tone, it sounded like he did. "And if it messes with my powers?"

He grabbed her hand and sobered. "Then we won't even try."

He was so accommodating. "Thank you." Rye slipped off his shirt and toed off his shoes. "What are you doing? I am not having sex in the open."

"Sex? Is that all you think about?" He winked.

He was such a liar. It was all he thought about. "Why are you getting naked then?"

Rye finished taking off his jeans. "Hurry." He jumped off the rock, crossed the path, and then dove into the water.

Was he kidding? With strong strokes, Rye swam toward the middle of the lake and dove down under. When he failed to surface within thirty seconds, Izzy rushed to the edge of the water. "Rye?"

Even though her hands were shaking, she lifted them then widened her arms in an attempt to part the lake. As the water fell away, Rye surfaced about ten feet from where she'd performed her magic.

"What are you doing?" he asked with a hint of fear in his tone.

She immediately motioned for the lake to fill back in. "I thought you might be drowning."

Rye returned close to shore then grinned. "You were worried about me, weren't you?"

It wouldn't hurt to tell him that much. "Yes."

"Come on in and show me how concerned you really were. The water's great."

Did he really think she'd take off her clothes out there? "I'm good."

"No you aren't. You need to cut lose. What are you afraid of?" Rye stepped out of the water and droplets cascaded down his glorious body, and her every need surfaced. As if someone else was guiding her hand, Izzy stepped out of her shoes and pants.

Rye neared. "Keep going."

"Or what?"

"You're going in that water with or without clothes."

Izzy was never this spontaneous. *No time like the present.* With Rye inches in front of her, she discarded her top. Wearing only her bra and panties she looked around but spotted no one. "Are any wolves around that you can sense?"

His gaze never left her face. "No."

Here goes. She took off her bra and Rye's eyes turned that gorgeous golden-green when he was aroused, and his cock stood firm at attention. "No sex in the lake, okay?" she said.

He laughed. "Where's the fun in that?"

"Rye!"

"The longer you take, the weaker I become. It's so damn hard to resist you. You have no idea how much I want you."

She hadn't meant to be a tease. Inhaling deeply, Izzy stepped out of her panties and his grin widened. In a flash, she was in his arms and then in the lake.

"It's cold," she said, though pressing against Rye's warm body helped somewhat.

"I'll show you cold."

Holding her in his arms, he dove down but surfaced quickly. As soon as she was able to breathe again, she twisted around and straddled him while Rye treaded water. "What if I couldn't swim?" she asked.

"Not to worry. I wasn't going to let go of you."

She smiled. "Race you to that tree over there." It was about fifty feet from them.

"You like losing, don't you?" he asked with way too much sass.

It was one sport she actually enjoyed. She could swim by herself and not be taunted by others. "You chicken?"

"What do I get when I win?" he asked.

"A kiss."

"A kiss could lead to other things."

"Only if you win." Before they had the chance to seal the deal, Izzy took off.

When Rye grabbed her leg from behind then shot past her, she had no choice but to use a little magic. With a big exhale, she created several large waves on Rye's side that caused him slow down.

She was laughing so hard at his attempt to win that she nearly lost. Rye caught up with her one second later. "You will pay for cheating."

"I didn't cheat."

"Did too." Rye drew her close then tickled her.

Barely able to reach the bottom, Izzy grabbed his hands to stop him, but she couldn't catch her breath. "I give."

Rye stopped, gathered her in his arms, and walked out of the lake with her. "I'll have to teach you a lesson about playing fair."

Given the way his incisors had elongated and his scruff had sprouted, she was going to love that lesson.

Chapter Fifteen

RYE CARRIED IZZY back to where they'd stripped and set her down. "We'll need our clothes."

About time he came to his senses. She picked them up. Putting jeans on while she was wet wouldn't be pleasant, but she certainly wasn't planning on walking back to his house naked. Before she could put anything on, Rye took her hand and led her to his rock. Instead of climbing on top, he half dragged her behind it.

"Drop your clothes," he commanded.

The intensity of his gaze heated her from the inside out, so she did. "Now what?"

"Take your punishment." With one arm, he pulled her close. "I plan to torment you with kisses and touches."

She laughed. "Oh, let the torture begin."

"I don't want you to move," he commanded. "I don't know how long I'm going to last, but I'm going to try."

This time she didn't ask what would happen if she did. Instead of the deep, soul-penetrating kiss she expected, he dropped to his knees and spread her legs wide. Goose bumps raced up her arms and legs in anticipation, though it was possible the air was cooling her wet body.

Rye didn't move as he stared at her naked form. "Stop stalling," she said.

Rye raised his head, his eyes almost glowing. Uh-oh, pushing him might cause an unwanted shift. While she doubted her eyes had changed color, Izzy was convinced something in her was different. His mere touch sent her desires to new heights, and his scent had already invaded her body. It had a magical element all its own.

"Prepare to be ravished," he said.

True to his word, the first swipe of his tongue had her clamping down hard on his head, and waves of euphoria spread across her like ripples of water on the surface of the lake.

"That feels so good."

Rye slipped a finger into her, and she rose up on her toes, trying to catch her breath. When he hit her G-spot, she almost came. Begging him to take her right then might push him over the edge, and she wanted them both to last.

To her delight and dismay, he sucked on her clit just as she was attempting to gain some control. It was too much, too intense, too exciting. Her whole body shimmered blue as her climax swooped down and claimed her. Her near scream had a few birds taking flight, which was exactly what her heart was doing—flying away with joy.

Rye stood and grinned. "You liked that?"

She cupped the scruff on his face. "Not at all. You'll have to work a little harder next time."

Rye drew her closer until their wet chests were plastered against each other. The kiss that followed was demanding, powerful, and so full of passion her knees weakened. A second later, her feet left the ground and she was forced to wrap her legs around his waist or chance slipping out of his grasp.

Together, he walked them over to the pile of clothes on the rock, adeptly snatched his shirt from the heap, and placed it over her shoulder. "Protection."

She wasn't sure what he meant until he backed her up to the rock slab.

Rye broke the kiss. "I want you so damn bad."

"And I want you." As much as she really wanted to suck on his cock, she wanted him inside her more.

Rye pounced and kissed her again, then trailed his kisses down her neck before scraping his teeth along the shell of her left earlobe. How that little act could make her so wet, she didn't know.

Tempted to help guide him into her, she couldn't gain any traction on his legs. Darn.

"I've got you," he said. Lifting her with one arm, he aimed his cock at her entrance then slowly eased her down.

Lust descended, and she realized she needed him more than life itself. Naliana must be above guiding them because all hell broke loose as soon as he filled her. With her arms around his neck, Izzy dove at his mouth, and their tongues entwined. Breath for breath, they joined as one, and as Rye plunged into her even deeper, sparks lit her up from the inside out. Her blue glow grew and grew until it cocooned both of them into one bright shell of light.

This was it. She would finally mate with Rye. Izzy lowered her head and sucked on his shoulder as he pounded into her. The blood pulsing in her head blocked out the sounds of the world, and nothing mattered but Rye.

His grip tightened, and when he filled her to the hilt, another orgasm threatened to descend. As if the world might end tomorrow, they fucked each other with a wild fierceness born from being mates for life. His teeth dug into her shoulder just as his hot seed heated her insides, and she swallowed her scream as her orgasm claimed her. Rye's grunts and groans seemed to come from deep in his chest, and he didn't seem to care that he made enough noise for every shifter around to hear.

They were now mates in the truest sense.

When his dick stopped pulsing, Izzy lowered her legs to the ground and sagged against him. "Why can't I ever seem to get my fill of you?" she asked.

"That's what happens when you find the perfect mate."

"How true."

He nibbled her neck. "You've made me a very happy man, my mate."

His touch was turning her on again. "I'm the one who's happy. I never thought I'd ever find someone who understands me like you do."

He lifted his head and kissed her briefly. "That means a lot to me. Perhaps we should take another dip to clean up. Because if we don't, I have to take you again."

She laughed. "Is it always going to be like this?"

He grinned. "I hope so."

"Wait. Turn around. I want to see if your marking has changed."

When she saw the vine laced through his paw, she ran a finger down his marking. "It's beautiful."

Rye whipped around. "Alphas don't have beautiful marks."

Izzy laughed. "You have a very masculine addition to the paw print then." She grinned when he grunted.

"You ready to take that dip?"

Since she was already wet, she wouldn't mind rinsing. "Can you check first that we're alone?"

He tapped her nose. "I keep forgetting how shy you are."

Izzy lifted her chin. "I think what we just did proves I'm quite adventurous."

"You're right. You are."

After they had a refreshing dip, they dressed then returned to the house, discussing what she needed to do in the coming days and weeks to remain safe. While she appreciated his concern, Rye was becoming more possessive than ever, but she kind of liked it. No one had ever looked out for her interests like he did.

He pulled two bottles of water from the fridge then sat with her at the dining room table. Izzy downed half the bottle then waved it at him. "Just so you know, I'm not going to stop living my life because of a crazy man. Having to look over my shoulder every minute of the day would drive me crazy. Besides, my powers are restored, which means I can handle him."

"You trying to convince yourself or me?" Rye scooted his chair closer and ran his hands down her shoulders. "Look, if this Owen Chancellor guy is still in town, it means he's planning another attack.

I imagine he paid a nice chunk of change to have a Changeling witch give him a spell. He won't stop now."

She blew out a breath, her shoulders sagging. "I know you believe he won't leave until he has me, but how does he plan to accomplish that?"

"Ophelia said the spell can be reinitiated after twenty-four hours have passed."

That was true. "Which is tomorrow," she said.

Rye wrapped his arms around her. "Don't worry. I'll protect you."

She leaned back. "You can't be everywhere. You have a job, and you have to prepare to take over the Clan's leadership role."

He cupped her face. "You are more important to me than anything else—the Clan included."

She swallowed hard. As much as she liked hearing how much he cared for her, she wished she understood the source of his desire. Did being mates alone create his need? Or was it that he respected and perhaps even loved her a little?

"A penny for your thoughts," he said.

She painted on a smile. "Just trying to come to grips with all of this."

"I know just the thing to help." He grabbed her hand and placed it on his crotch.

Izzy laughed. "Sex is not the solution to all problems. In case you forgot, we just made love at your favorite spot."

"So? I'll never have enough of you."

She needed to redirect his one-track mind. "While I find your infinite need for me highly flattering, how do you think your parents will react when they found out you mated with a Wendayan?"

In a flash, he pushed back his chair, leaned over, and pulled her onto his lap before wrapping an arm snuggly around her. "My parents will be thrilled. Remember, our folks are friends. Joining the two groups will be good for us all. When I'm the Alpha, I want to see better communication between the *Weres* and the Wendayans."

"Is that what this is about—you creating a bigger kingdom?"

"That is so far from the truth I'm unable to even address it." He drew her close and pressed her face against his shoulder. Warmth and comfort surrounded her.

She sat back up. "You have to admit it sounded that way."

"It did and I'm sorry. I'm used to shooting pool, gambling, drinking, and having fun times with the guys. To be honest, I'm thirty-two and have never had a real relationship before, because I knew every woman I asked out wasn't my mate. I'm going to suck at this being a couple stuff for a while, so will you be patient with me?"

His honesty touched her. Should she tell him the truth that she'd be willing to wait a long time, or tease him just a little?

"That depends on how good you are."

A second later, she was in the air headed to the bedroom. Oh, boy. She never knew being a mate would lead to this.

"YOU NERVOUS?" RYE asked as he pulled into his parents' drive for the party.

"Should I be? It's not like they don't know me." He raised his brows. "Okay, fine. Yes, I'm a bit nervous."

"I promise you there will be squeals of excitement when they see us together," he said.

"I'm glad they know." He'd called them this afternoon and told them. "Shocking relatives is never good." He held open her car door. "Before we go in, tell me who's going to be there. I don't want to call someone by the wrong name."

Rye rubbed her arm. "Just the family—except for my brother Devon who is out of town at the other security office. Besides Chelsea, I'm assuming Connor and Finn will be there." He slipped the dessert from her hands. "That's heavy."

"It's a jumbo peach cobbler. I wasn't sure how many guests to bake for."

He inhaled. "It smells wonderful. My parents will love it."

She hoped so. They entered through the front, but everyone had gathered in the backyard. He set the cobbler on the kitchen counter and escorted her outside.

Chairs were scattered in a haphazard manner around the endless back yard that was filled with oak and pine trees. Connor, who she hadn't seen in ages, was sitting with Finn. As soon as he spotted them he jumped up, came over, and hugged her. "Izzy, you're looking good."

"Thank you." In high school, she had been a bit dumpy and had no boobs—still didn't have much now. Add in braces and wild, crazy hair and she wasn't anyone who could attract a man back then, even if she'd wanted to. Thankfully, her hair had tamed down a bit as she grew older, and she'd shed those unwanted pounds.

Even though Connor had only been a year ahead of her in school, they hadn't interacted much. Always fearing people would find out about her talents, Izzy spent her time hiding in the science lab, while Connor, Mr. Outgoing, loved showing off his prowess on the sports field.

After high school, she'd headed off to college. When she returned home for two years before traipsing off to Europe, she'd spotted him around town, but they'd rarely spoken. Shifters and Wendayans, while cordial with each other, were in a totally different place emotionally. Wendayans tended to be more reserved, whereas most of the shifters were free spirits.

"There you are," Rye's mom said as she barreled down on them. She held Izzy out at arm's length. "Haven't you grown up to be a beauty. My son is one lucky man."

She wasn't used to all of this attention and painted on her best smile. "Thank you."

When Rye had told his family they were mated, he'd also mentioned some of her talents, but hopefully they wouldn't ask her to demonstrate her magic.

Chelsea had led them to believe that this was a welcome home party, but it seemed to be more of a meet-the-new-girlfriend affair instead.

Rye wrapped an arm around her shoulder. "Let's go say hi to the twins."

That would be Chelsea and Finn.

"We'll talk later," Mrs. McKinnon said.

"That wasn't nice," she telepathed him.

"Mom would have drilled you with questions. She probably wanted to make sure you aren't some gold digger."

Izzy cracked up. "I do fine on my own." Izzy stopped then twisted to face him. "Are you rich or something?"

Rye squeezed her waist then let go. "I do fine on my own."

She grinned. "Funny man."

When they approached his youngest brother, Finn popped up and shook her hand. "I see my brother didn't scare you off after playing pool with you."

She leaned closer and whispered. "I let him win."

Finn guffawed. "Next time you come to the Pub I want to watch."

"I'd have to cheat, and I doubt that would go over too well with the locals."

His brows rose. "Cheat, how so?"

Even though she wasn't there to show off, in this case a demonstration would be best. Finn, who appeared to be the most carefree of the group, would take her little show for what it was. Chelsea's rescued puppy was running around the yard, playing with an old tennis ball. At the moment, the ratty ball was sitting idle about three feet from the dog. Izzy held up her hand and created enough wind to move the yellow object ten feet farther away. Badger barked, ran after it, and then pounced. He looked around as if trying to find out who'd thrown it.

Finn clapped. "That's so cool. Do something else."

She twisted around and motioned with her hand for the wind to blow the tree limb behind Finn. It slapped him in the head. He jumped, and then both Rye and Chelsea burst out laughing.

Rye's parents, along with Connor, sauntered over. Mrs. McKinnon had a smile on her face. "I wish I could do that. Why if I had that talent back when these kids were young, my life would have been a whole lot easier."

Resorting to magic for discipline purposes never seemed right. "It's too hard to use in public without attracting attention though."

She wrinkled her nose. "I'd find a way. My life was rather hectic with five kids in eight years. Looking back on all that chaos still shoots up my blood pressure. I don't know how Cam talked me into having so many."

Mr. McKinnon moved closer to his wife. "We were young mates in love. Don't you remember how you kept me tied to the bed for months on end?"

Rye's face reddened. "Not appropriate, Dad."

"She's a big girl. If Izzy is going to be a part of the family, she'll have to get used to our kind of humor."

"Dad, Izzy may be my mate, but we need to give her some breathing room."

"Thank you."

His father's face actually reddened. "Sorry Izzy. It's just that Celia and I are so excited that Rye chose you, or rather that you two were fated mates."

Mrs. McKinnon held out her hand. "You want to help me in the kitchen? I know the boys must be starving."

Izzy appreciated the save. "I'd love to."

Once inside, Rye's mom turned to her. "I want to apologize for Cameron. He was so excited when we learned you and Rye mated. I think my husband's remembering our courting days and how rough it was on him. He never wanted his own kids to deal with the prejudice."

"What do you mean?"

Mrs. McKinnon leaned against the counter. "I don't talk about it much, but my mother was pure wolf while my father was a mixed breed—part wolf, part bear. Cam's father was rather upset that his fated mate was someone who wasn't one hundred percent wolf."

"Like me."

"Enough talk about being different. I'm just happy you're going to be part of the family."

"Me too."

"Okay then, there's a tray in the refrigerator with the hamburger patties and hotdogs. How about taking them out to Cam, and I'll take out the potato salad and chips?"

"Can do." That went a lot better than she could ever have imagined. Izzy picked up the tray out and carried it outside.

Oh, my. Three wolves were playing with the puppy, or should she say tormenting the little thing? One wolf would grab the ball then drop it twenty feet away. When the puppy chased after it, a second wolf would steal it. The puppy barked and the wolves howled. Growing up, she and her family never let loose like this. It was as if someone feared they'd release their powers by mistake.

Cam McKinnon was at the grill, so she carried the tray of meat over to him. "Special delivery."

Rye's dad nodded to his sons and sighed. "They have so much fun together. I love when everyone's here. It's a shame Devon couldn't come."

She and Missy had loved to play dress-up and pretend they ran the household, but somehow, this family seemed to revel in fun. Rye slowed and lifted his nose in the air as if he had detected something.

He then suddenly shifted back into his human form—and oh my, he was naked. He looked over at her and smiled.

Only then did it occur to her that when Connor and Finn shifted too, they'd be in the same state of undress, and she wasn't ready to see that. Izzy wasn't sure when or if she could get used to such a blatant display of nakedness. Chelsea seemed to be the smart one. She'd turned her back to the whole affair.

In wolf form, Connor and Finn chased one another toward the side of the house and disappeared with the puppy at their heels. Just then Rye's mom came out with another tray of food. Rye took one look at her and his smile disappeared.

"Ryerson Cameron McKinnon. You should be ashamed of yourself. You get dressed this minute. Izzy doesn't need to see you like that."

His wide-eyed look cracked up Izzy. Rye turned and sprinted to the side of the house where he must have left his clothes. She faced his mom. "It sure seems to me, Mrs. McKinnon, that you don't need any magic to keep your sons in line."

She chuckled. "Maybe not. Seeing you are truly part of the family, it's time you call me Celia."

"Celia it is." Right then and there they bonded.

Connor and Finn waltzed back toward the party, fully dressed, but Rye was nowhere to be seen. Seconds later, he appeared and called over his two brothers. Connor nodded and then he ducked out of sight while Rye and Finn returned. What was that all about?

When Rye came up to her, she clasped his arm and pulled him out of earshot of his parents. "What's going on?"

"What do you mean?"

She glanced upward. "I saw how you sniffed the air. Then you were gone a long time to change."

Rye rubbed her shoulder. "Sorry. I thought I detected another wolf, but when I searched, no one was there."

"But you sent Connor to look too?"

Rye leaned over and kissed her. "Just a precaution, my love."

She sighed. No one could get to her with Rye there to protect her.

WHAT A DISGUSTING *display of family unity.* If they'd been in Scotland, the McKinnons would have been ousted if they had acted like that, and Isadora, really? Showing off her magic like that was unacceptable.

She bent down to pet the dog that had returned from the side, and her shirt twisted, exposing the marking on her left shoulder blade. Only this time it had the sign of a paw on top of her vines, and Owen saw red. She and Ryerson had mated! No, no, no.

Stay calm.

The future Alpha of his Clan would not be thwarted by this setback. Isadora was not a shifter. He could change her mind. All he needed was a little help.

Chapter Sixteen

THE NEXT MORNING, Rye had to be up bright and early, and as much as Izzy wanted to sleep in, Rye needed a ride into work as he'd returned his dad's car to him. Rye told her he'd pick up his vehicle after work.

Still a bit sleepy, Izzy hauled herself out of bed, threw on a pair of jeans and a T-shirt, and hopped into the driver's seat. She turned the engine over and sighed. "I'm glad I have today off. I don't think I'd be very effective working on clients."

Rye ran a hand down her arm. "I'm sorry the family tired you out. We can be rather loud and crazy."

She glanced over at him. "I think it was all the sex beforehand that did it."

He chuckled and then puffed out his chest. "If you plan to stay with me baby, you better get used to it."

Oh, boy, he made her laugh at his sex-driven mind. "Truthfully, your family's carefree nature was what I liked the best. Wait until you're at one of my family affairs. They're rather sedate."

"I'm sure they're not that bad."

"You'd be surprised," she said. When he smiled, his lively eyes boosted her energy.

"What are your plans for the day?" While his tone came out light, there was an undertone of concern.

"Don't worry. I won't go anywhere. There's plenty of food in the house, so I won't need to go out. I might take a walk around the lake, but that's all."

He'd previously told her that if Owen Chancellor entered their community, his powers would be diminished, though she had no idea why. She suspected it had something to do with a pact made long ago with Naliana or James.

"If no fires break out, I'll be home for dinner. Maybe we could watch a movie, and this time I promise not to fall asleep."

He really seemed to want to do things together and she liked that. "I'll reserve judgment until after the movie is over."

When she pulled in front of the firehouse, Rye leaned over and kissed her. Whether it was the casual way his lips pressed against hers or his cheerful attitude, Izzy really wanted to turn the car around and take him back to bed—again. "See you tonight."

As soon as Rye disappeared into the station, a wave of depression descended, and Izzy wasn't quite sure how to handle the novel feeling. Her whole life, she'd been brought up to deal with issues head on, but love had never been in the mix.

Love. That was a word she never thought she'd have to deal with. What she had with Rye was different from anything she'd ever experienced. She thought about him all the time and wanted to be with him, so perhaps she was in love.

His house appeared all too quickly, but she was pleased that she'd arrived safely. Needing to be closer to Rye's energy, she decided to visit their rock. It seemed to bring Rye solace when he was growing up, so perhaps it would hold some magic for her as well.

The walk down the path in the fresh air and the bright sunshine, along with the rustling of leaves and the singing of birds, helped renew her spirit. When she came to the path that cut into the lake, she hurried along it. Something about this body of water drew her in like no other. She'd heard tales about its magic, but no one had ever told her what it entailed. She'd have to ask Rye about it tonight.

When she reached the rock, she climbed on top and let the tension in her shoulders release. Rye might be at work, but it sure felt as if his aura was there with her.

"Hello," said a voice from behind, startling her.

Izzy slapped a hand on her chest as her insides squeezed. Ready to throw some fire at the newcomer, she twisted around and immediately sagged when she saw it was James.

"You scared me."

"I'm sorry. May I?" He motioned to the spot next to her.

"Sure." She scooted over to give him room.

James climbed next to her, and once more, she marveled at how youthful he looked and how fluidly he moved. "You have something on your mind I see."

His insightful comment kind of creeped her out. After all, he was only a human—who just happened to be able to live forever. "What do you mean?"

He smiled. "Rye always came here when he had something on his mind. I sensed the same feeling from you."

Perhaps this was what others experienced when they saw her magic—that sense of how was it possible? Best if she didn't dissect James's abilities too closely. "What do you know about humans being able to shift after they mate?"

He leaned back on his elbows and nodded. "You want to know if the ability to shift will interfere with your extensive powers."

"Yes."

"And perhaps more importantly, how will it affect your children?"

"We haven't discussed kids yet, but yes, I have wondered about that. Do you think an offspring would have my powers as well as Rye's?" She wasn't sure she wanted to do that to a child. It was hard enough to hide her talents let alone be a shifter too. Then there were the issues of belonging to two different groups of people.

"I wish I could give you a definitive answer. It's been a long time since a Wendayan mated with a wolf. I do recall that the Wendayan's powers were nothing like yours though."

This conversation was only depressing her more. "Given that I can manipulate the elements, if I try to shift, can you guess the consequences?"

He picked up her hand, and his warmth and comfort surprised her. "I believe you will lose some of your powers after you shift, though not right away."

That wasn't what she wanted to hear. "Thank you for your honesty."

James nodded. As quickly as he came, he slipped off the rock and disappeared back into the forest.

Izzy lay on her back and studied the clouds morphing into different shapes as they passed overhead. While she appreciated the chance to speak with James, she was more confused than ever. It wasn't just about what she wanted, Rye's opinion counted equally.

Her mom would tell her not to even think about agreeing to shift if it meant losing her powers. What if James was wrong and her magic disappeared completely? She might not even be a Wendayan anymore. After all, a Wendayan was a human with magical powers. Mrs. McKinnon would probably tell her to do what was in her heart because her wonderful son would deal with the consequences.

Hell, Izzy wasn't even certain what she wanted to do. The sad thing was that she hadn't paid any attention to the phases of the moon and had no idea when the white moon would appear again. Whenever it was, she needed to be ready to make her decision— assuming it was up to her.

Moving tended to help her think more clearly, so she walked back to the path to continue her stroll around the lake. She'd never been around the entire perimeter and she figured there was no time like the present. Part of her allure to Rye, she believed, was her ability to perform magic. When he became the Alpha, she believed his people would respect her more if she had her powers. On the other hand, if she were a shifter, she'd be more like the rest of the Clan. Ugh. In the end, she needed to work this out with her mate.

After she finished her loop, she returned to his house. Izzy wasn't used to being cooped up for any length of time, but she understood why she needed to stay put. If she were at her house, she'd either be gardening or practicing her skills. With nothing to do, she searched the cabinets for a meal she could prepare. If she'd felt a bit more comfortable, she would have called his mom to find out what his favorite foods were.

This only highlighted how much she didn't know about him, but then she recalled that her parents had only known each other a few months before marrying. Her mother said the moment she set eyes on her dad, she knew he was the one. Izzy had to admit she felt the same way about Rye.

Around five, her cell rang. Her luck, she was in the middle of folding the eggs into the ground beef and quickly rinsed her hands. Putting the call on speaker, she answered. It was Rye.

"Hey there, did you get your car?"

"I did, but I'm afraid I was called back in to work. Two of the men on the next shift took sick, and I have to fill in for them."

Oh, crap. There was so much she wanted to discuss with him. "I was making meatloaf for you." That sounded so petty. Here Rye might have to work for twenty-four hours straight. "Never mind. I know it's your job."

He groaned. "I am so sorry. Don't wait up for me. I promise I'll make it up to you tomorrow."

"I'll be counting on it," she said in her most cheerful tone. Shouts sounded in the background. "Sounds like you need to go. Come to bed naked."

"You are a true witch. See you later."

After she hung up, Izzy's energy had improved just hearing Rye's voice.

IZZY VAGUELY REMEMBERED Rye returning last night, but then fell back asleep to the soothing sound of running water. When her alarm went off, his arms were entwined around her, and he smelled of lemon soap. Her mate looked so cute with his rough beard and messed up hair, and the soft snoring was more like a sleeping puppy than a big burly man.

So as not to wake him, Izzy slowly eased out from under his arms. He grunted a few times but didn't wake. Poor guy. Working so many hours straight had to be hard on the body. Just thinking about going into work today made her drag. She should be checking out teaching opportunities at the local schools since summer would be over before she knew it. Since both schools were a few miles outside of town, she decided it might be wiser to stay near the spa until after that Chancellor creep was caught.

If he did try to capture her again, he'd be in for a big surprise when he found her powers had returned. Rye had reminded her that the black witch who'd provided the spell might have told Chancellor its effects only lasted two days. In which case, Izzy really did have to be careful.

As she was dressing, she thought about one additional conse-quence of learning to shift. If her powers faded or disappeared at all, she might have to look over her shoulder for the rest of her life. On the other hand, if she became a shifter, she'd be able to sense when another shifter was near.

Izzy lightly kissed a sleeping Rye goodbye. "See you later," she whispered.

He snorted but didn't wake. When she arrived at the spa, Missy was getting things ready in front, and she could hear Teagan in the back. "Is Mom here?" Izzy asked.

"She had some errands to run first. We have three scheduled massages and that's all for today. The three of us can handle that." Missy headed off to the back.

Izzy hadn't had the chance to talk with Teagan yet after she had poked her head out of the back door and called for help. She snapped her fingers. Izzy had to remember to return the robe that Teagan had lent Rye.

The last few days had been a total whirlwind of activity, and she couldn't focus on more than one thing at a time.

Teagan emerged from the back and hugged her. "Hey, I haven't seen you since that terrible man grabbed you. Missy filled me in, but I want to hear how you're doing."

"I'm so sorry I didn't call and let you know, but I've been so caught up being with Rye and meeting his family. I'm fine, really."

"I heard you're staying with him. How's that going?"

"Different. Exciting and a bit challenging at times." That led to a host of questions that she answered with care.

"So you two are mated, for real?" Her cousin's eyes shone.

"For real."

"I'm so happy for you."

"Thanks. I do have a question for you," Izzy said.

"Shoot."

"Was it pure luck that you looked out the back door when you did?"

Teagan pressed her lips together and shook her head. "No. I was in the back room lighting some incense when my head started to pound."

"You had a premonition?"

"A really strong one; I saw a black cloud descend on the alley in the back. I wasn't sure what it meant, but I did know it was happening right then. I don't recall ever receiving an image that strong before. Usually, my premonitions are for the future—as in days or weeks. This was so intense I nearly vomited from the pain."

Izzy clasped her shoulder and rubbed it. "I'm so sorry."

She shook her head. "It's not your fault."

"It was in a way. I was the one being attacked."

"Don't be silly. I had to look out back. When I spotted that man with his hand over your mouth, all I could do was scream. I dialed 911 right away and then called Uncle Len. I figured since he was closer he might be able to stop that man."

"Thank you."

"I just wished someone could have caught the guy."

Izzy nodded. "They will."

The door opened and the chime sounded, though Izzy didn't

recognize the woman. Missy stepped from the back room. After greeting the newcomer, her sister led her to one of the rooms they used for massages. Teagan moved closer. "Something's troubling you. Can I help?"

Izzy almost chuckled. "I know you have premonitions, but can you read people's minds now too?"

"No, but you are my cousin, and you seem preoccupied."

Teagan had always been sensible and quite serious. Normally, Izzy would have gone to Elana with her concern, but it would have been too hard for a human with no powers to truly understand what it would mean to give up her identity.

"I would like to talk."

Teagan smiled. "I'm all ears."

Chapter Seventeen

A FEW MINUTES before lunch, Izzy's cell rang, and she hoped it was Rye asking if she wanted to go to lunch. After she retrieved her cell and swiped the screen to answer, she sighed then smiled answering, "Hey, Elana."

A trickle of guilt surfaced. Izzy had texted Elana telling her that Rye was back to normal after one day's rest but nothing about that walk along Silver Lake. Mostly it was because Izzy didn't want to whine about possibly losing her powers when Elana didn't have any to begin with.

"I was wondering if you wanted to go to lunch?" asked Elana. "We were interrupted the other day if you recall."

Getting away would be awesome. "I'd love to as long as it's Nate's Pizzeria or the Silver Lake Café. I don't want to be wandering about for too long. No telling who might be lurking."

"That's smart. How about Silver Lake Café in thirty minutes? I have to run a few errands first."

"I can't wait. See you there!"

Missy came up behind her. "Hot date with Rye?"

"That was Elana. She asked me to lunch, and I said yes. Rye doesn't want me to leave his compound, and Mom doesn't want me to leave the store, so I'm going stir-crazy."

Missy tilted her head in her typical sympathetic manner. "Your stalker is getting to you, isn't he?"

"Every once in a while, but it's nothing I can't handle."

Just as Missy opened her mouth, the conversation was cut short when two elderly women wandered in wearing *I Love Tennessee* T-shirts. "I got this," she told Missy. "May I help you, ladies?" Izzy asked.

"Why yes." They were curious about the purpose of the pretty crystals in the storefront window. One of the ladies then wanted to know if there was a candle scent to help with her headaches. By the time Izzy explained what each crystal was used for, along with the benefits of aromatherapy, the ladies had taken up twenty of her thirty-minute window, setting her nerves on edge. They'd purchased two candles apiece, and once she rang them up, she only had five minutes to reach the café. Teagan was with a client, so Izzy told Missy she'd be back in an hour.

"Have fun."

Being late grated on her, but she couldn't leave her customers in the middle of a transaction. Izzy snatched her purse and rushed out. Silver Lake Café was on the same street as the spa and only two and a half blocks away. As much as she wanted to enjoy the clear, balmy day, Izzy didn't want to keep her friend waiting. Elana had a flower shop to run.

Just as she passed Thomas's Hardware, someone stepped out from the between the buildings. So focused on reaching the café in time, she hadn't checked to see if the alleyway was clear.

He pressed something hard into her back. "Don't scream, lass, or I'll shoot 'cha."

Bile rose to her throat. Owen Chancellor had found her, and he had a gun. Shit. *Think. Think. Do something.*

Izzy could lift her hand and shoot fire behind her, but that might catch her on fire as well. Being on the sidewalk, she couldn't make a plant grow to ensnare him, but there had to be something she could do that wouldn't attract too much attention. Creating a windstorm might distract him, but it wouldn't stop a bullet.

With his left hand, he grabbed her arm and told her to walk down Oak Avenue. Her mind spun. Except for an older gentleman across the street using a cane, the road was devoid of traffic.

He nudged her back. "Open that car door and get in."

If she could move far enough away from him, she might be able to use her magic to thwart him. Feeling confident there would be a window of opportunity to take him down, Izzy complied. As he rushed over to the driver's side, she considered jumping out and running, but she believed her stalker when he said he'd shoot.

He started the car then pulled onto the road, thankfully not insisting she fasten her seatbelt. Izzy wanted to be able to escape if he stopped. He hadn't blindfolded her either, which was another stroke of luck. She'd be able to tell when it was safe to use her magic.

Chancellor headed north out of town on Pine View Avenue. As soon as he turned on Grand Peak Drive, taking them into the mountains, dread pooled in her stomach. This was Changeling territory.

"Where are you taking me?" she demanded.

"We're going to have a little ceremony."

Her blood ran cold. What kind of ceremony? Marriage, sacrificial, or some other demonic torture? The big question was whether he needed her alive.

Without warning, Chancellor jerked the car down a dirt road that seemed to lead nowhere. The jarring caused her to hit her head on the roof twice. He then stopped.

"Get out," he commanded.

Was this it? Had he brought her to this desolate part of town so he could kill her then dump her body? Poor Rye. A wolf without his mate would end horribly for him.

With trembling hands, she lifted the door latch while trying to devise the best plan to kill him. Running, however, wasn't an option. He'd shift and catch her quickly, making her death painful.

Owen Chancellor popped the trunk then slid out with his gun in his hand. "I'm sorry to have to do this, but I need you to get in the back. I can't have you see where we're going."

While he didn't intend to kill her right away, riding in the trunk of a car was only slightly more appealing. "No way I'm getting in there."

Up to this point, she'd been compliant, but this was as far as it went. Just as Izzy lifted her hand to send a blast of wind strong enough to knock him down, he raised his arm and fired. Her arm kicked to the side and the wind she'd sent blew down a tree near him, missing her captor by yards.

A second later, her brain registered the pain in her upper arm, and it sucked the air right out of her lungs. Izzy glanced down at the blood pouring out, and disbelief slammed into her. "You shot me."

Her stomach convulsed, but she wouldn't be thwarted. Izzy lifted her uninjured arm, needing to incinerate the bastard now. Before she had the chance to send off a burning blast, a second shot grazed her hip, buckling her left knee. She dropped to the ground.

Chancellor strode toward her and then kicked her in the stomach. She couldn't breathe.

"Now get in the trunk or I'll shoot ya in the belly, 'cause if I can't have ya then no one's gonna have ya."

"You fucking bastard. What do you want?" She'd tried to shout but the words came out in spurts.

He bent down, picked her up, and then dumped her in the trunk. Excruciating pain traveled up her spine and nearly made her cry out. The moment the lid shut, Izzy lifted her good arm and banged on the roof, but it did no good.

RYE WAS WORKING hard to stay focused. The call from his supervisor an hour ago had been urgent but apologetic. One of the local elementary schools had been deliberately set on fire, and he was needed to help with the blaze. What kind of bastard would do that? He could guess—a Changeling. Only why?

With only a few hours' sleep, his energy was waning, but he'd give it his best. The hoses were blasting out water at a rapid rate, and in the last few minutes, the fire had finally lost its strength. The administrators had evacuated all of the children, and thank goddess there had been no reported injuries. The only issue now was how much of the gym could be saved.

A sharp pain stabbed him in the arm, followed by an ache in his leg. What the hell? His pulse sped up as dread slowly seeped in. Was his mate in trouble?

Frank, his supervisor, rushed over waving his cell. "Got an emergency call for you," he shouted over the roar of the blaze and the rush of water.

If it hadn't been for Rye's excellent hearing and his ability to read lips, he never would have understood the message. Rye couldn't figure out who would be calling for him on his supervisor's phone. Not Izzy. Frank was suited up and motioned for Rye to hand him the hose.

"Thanks." Rye slipped the cell from his boss's fingers, turned his back to the blaze, and answered. "Hello?"

"Rye, it's Elana."

Had she not sounded so scared, he would have told her this was not a good time. "What's wrong?" *Please don't tell me something has happened to Izzy.*

"Izzy never showed up for our lunch date. I tried calling your cell, but you didn't answer. I had to call the station. I'm sorry."

"That's okay." Tension nearly crippled him, but he tried to stay positive. With all that had been on Izzy's mind, he prayed she'd forgotten the time of their date. Unfortunately, that didn't jive with the sharp jab to his arm a leg that he feared came from his mate. "When did you speak with her last?"

"An hour ago." She then explained where and when they were supposed to meet. "I've called her cell a few times, but it goes to voicemail."

He turned his attention away from Elana and tried to make contact with his mate. *"Izzy, can you hear me,"* he telepathed. After waiting three breaths for her to answer, he refocused on Izzy's friend. Rye's head pounded. "Elana, call me on my cell immediately if Izzy contacts you, okay?"

"I promise, and please let me know when you find her." Elana sucked in a breath as if she was close to hyperventilating.

"I will."

Once more, he attempted to connect with Izzy, but again, he didn't receive a response. His gut twisted into multiple knots, and his heart beat faster than a hummingbird's. He rushed back to Frank and returned his phone. "I'm sorry, my fiancée has been kidnapped." Calling Izzy his mate would not have been wise.

Frank's eyes widened, though Rye didn't have time to find out if it was because he hadn't known Rye had a fiancée, or that someone he knew had been kidnapped.

"Go. We have the blaze under control. Thanks for helping out."

Rye was grateful he didn't have to argue about taking off before the fire was out. After leaving his suit in the truck, he rushed back to his SUV, his mind spinning. If Owen Chancellor had taken her, where would he go?

Rye rarely ventured into the hills, mostly because the Change-lings lived there, but he'd have to head there now. Damn. Chancellor had sought out a black witch once, so he might try her again. Too bad Rye had no idea who she was or where she lived.

"James," he blurted. He'd know.

The immortal had mentioned his contact had found out Owen Chancellor's name. Perhaps that person could provide him with the locations of the black witches. Rye jumped into his car, and as he sped down Oak Avenue toward High Point Street, he telepathed Kalan.

"I need your help. I think Izzy's been kidnapped."

"Give me the details." Thankfully, Kalan must have sensed time was of the essence and didn't question his statement. Rye spit out what he knew. *"I'm on my way to James's house to see if he can help. I'll let you know what he says."* Rye hadn't had the time to brief his best friend about his recent meeting with Naliana's husband. He needed to do a better job at communicating, especially with his Beta.

"I'll put an APB out on his vehicle."

"Thanks. I'll contact you if I find out more."

Rye's tires squealed as he turned onto the road toward the lake. While it wasn't more than two miles to his cottage, it seemed like a million miles away. Rye attempted to reach Izzy telepathically again, and after he thought he'd made a connection, all he received was what sounded like moans, and his heart pinched at the implication.

"Come on Izzy. Talk to me, baby. I know you can hear me."

"Rye."

Yes! His grip loosened on the wheel, but he didn't slow in case Izzy couldn't tell him her location.

"Where are you? Are you okay?" He finally let out a breath.

"Trun—Ow."

He had no idea why her words faded in and out. "Izzy, concentrate. Tell me where you are."

"Don't know."

"Did Chancellor take you?"

"Yes."

"Hold on. I'll find you." He then broke the connection. She'd sounded weak, and he didn't want her to waste her energy.

James's cabin came into view. Once in his driveway, Rye jammed the SUV into park, cut the engine, and hauled ass to the front door. He pounded until his host answered.

The door opened. "Come in, Rye. Tell me what's wrong." The man was the epitome of calm.

Rye was barely able to get the words out. "Izzy's in trouble. I think Owen Chancellor has her."

James led him over to the sofa. "Slow down and tell me everything."

Here he thought the man had super human powers and would already be aware of what had transpired. As coherently as he could, Rye imparted only the most important pieces of information. "Can you ask your source for the location of their witches?"

"I can try, but there's no guarantee Izzy is there. Seems to me this Chancellor person has an agenda we're not even sure about."

"I need to start somewhere."

As if Izzy were resting comfortably somewhere sipping tea instead of being held against her will, James eased up from the chair and went in search of his cell phone. Rye wanted to shake him at his lack of urgency.

"Here it is." James held up his cell and dialed someone. He explained what he needed and then listened for at least a minute. "Thank you."

He returned to his seat. "There are two witches that my source said might have dealt with your stalker." He wrote down their names and addresses. "I hope you know your way around the hills, as addresses are not well marked."

"I'll find it." *With Izzy's help.*

Rye ran out without thanking James. Damn. Once in the SUV, he dialed Izzy's cell, hoping she had her phone with her, but it went to voicemail as Elana had said. In case Chancellor had confiscated it, he didn't leave a message.

"Izzy, I'm going to find you. Hang in there."

"Hurry." The communication was much clearer this time. She sounded stronger, and the tightness in his throat relaxed somewhat.

"Can you tell me anything about your location?"

"In the trunk of Chancellor's car."

Acid burned a hole in his heart. *"Kalan and I will find you. If you learn anything, let me know."*

"Rye?"

"Yes."

"I love you."

"I love you too. Hang in there."

"I'm trying, but I've been shot."

With that news, Rye nearly ran off the road.

Chapter Eighteen

WHILE IZZY WAS relieved Rye knew she'd been kidnapped, she wasn't sure it would do her any good. The hole in her arm seemed to have stopped bleeding, but the wound to her hip was killing her—literally and figuratively. Every bump sent spikes of pain up her spine, and from the amount of the liquid on the carpet, she was losing blood rather quickly.

Damn. Why hadn't she thought to contact him when Chancellor shoved that gun in her back? Because she'd been overwhelmed and this whole telepathy thing was so new to her.

Rye's comment came back to her about how she'd have improved healing powers, but if that were true, why was she still in such pain? Was it because she needed to shift first? Unfortunately, that was out of her control. What she wouldn't give for her sister's healing ways now.

Needing to focus on escaping, she concentrated on what she'd have to do next. When Chancellor opened the trunk again, assuming he would, she'd have to use her magic on him from a prone position, as she was in no shape to jump out and attack. Fire seemed her best solution, but her aim when she was healthy was poor at best. Sadly, shooting fire didn't happen instantaneously, and she doubted he'd stand there while she created the heat.

If he were pointing a gun at her, she'd have to do as he said.

Izzy closed her eyes and pictured Rye sitting on the rock overlooking Silver Lake, hoping to reestablish the connection. In her weakened state, she wasn't sure she could communicate. *"Rye, where are you?"*

"Trying...you."

She wished she understood how this mental communication really worked, because the connection was so weak. The trunk opened and Izzy froze.

"Fuck. You bled on the carpet."

The rental car company would have a field day with that. "It wasn't *my* fault."

He reached in to grab her, but she waved him off. "I'll get out by myself." *Even if it kills me.*

Chancellor aimed his gun at her heart. "No shenanigans or I'll shoot you dead this time."

She believed him. A door opened, and footsteps sounded. "What's going on here?" It was a woman's voice and hope surged.

"Isadora isn't feeling well. Can you do the spell from there?" her captor asked.

Another spell? Her stomach cramped. She'd be helpless if her magic was taken from her again.

Suddenly, a young woman moved in front of the trunk, blocking the piercing sunlight. The backlight haloed her long black hair, but her facial features were in the shadows.

"She's injured. We need to get her inside. I'm not doing anything until her wounds are tended to."

When Izzy tried to sit up, she had to swallow the pain to keep from crying out. She ached in places other than where she'd been shot. Picturing Rye, Izzy pushed up and gasped.

The woman leaned over and placed her hands under Izzy's back. "Move her right leg," the woman commanded to the man.

With a grunt, Chancellor flung Izzy's leg over the side of the trunk lip. *Asshole.* "I can do it myself," Izzy said.

Between the woman's supporting arm and Izzy's sheer determination, she managed to stand, but as soon as she stepped on her bad leg, her knee buckled.

"You need to carry her," the woman said.

He waved his gun. "No way, she'll use her magic on me."

"I'm too weak," Izzy said. "My magic won't work." A blatant lie, but she was desperate.

The woman huffed, wrapped an arm around Izzy's waist, and guided her toward the double-wide trailer. The outside was gray vinyl, but the twelve by ten foot porch looked to be a makeshift add-on. The lady helped her up the three steps. Why was this woman being so nice? Rumors had it that all Changelings were bad. Perhaps a few had caused the hype.

Once inside, the woman guided her to a chair. "I'll get a towel. I don't want blood on my floor."

So much for altruism. The interior was sparse. What there was of it was mismatched furniture of poor quality. The only visible room was the living room they passed through and a dining room. A door off to the left probably led to the kitchen.

Owen Chancellor withdrew two pairs of handcuffs from his back pocket and leaned close. "Can't chance you doing something."

He yanked her arms behind her and snapped the cuffs closed, causing her to swallow a scream. Shit that hurt. Not only was her arm throbbing, without her hands, Izzy was powerless.

"Rye, can you hear me?" Crap, she forgot to focus on his image first. Staring straight ahead, she pictured how adorable he was encased in rumpled sheets this morning. _"Rye?"_

"I'm here," he replied right away. _"I'm sensing a lot of pain."_ The worry in his voice tore her up.

He could feel her ache? _"I'm okay. Chancellor has me handcuffed inside someone's house. A woman in her mid-twenties with long, straight black hair seems to own the place."_

"I'll find you."

A hard slap across her face stunned her back to the present and she let out a loud grunt. Tears brimmed on her lashes, but she wouldn't cry in front of him.

"Izzy?" Rye's plea tore at her heart.

"I'm okay." From the way her fear reached out to him, it wouldn't matter what she told him. He'd know the truth.

"Pay attention," Chancellor commanded.

To what?

The woman cleared her throat then pressed a dishtowel over Izzy's hip wound. Another piercing ache stabbed her and her breathing turned ragged. "That should help," the witch said. "The bleeding on your arm seems to have stopped."

"Thank you."

The witch stepped behind the table then lit four white candles. She carefully measured out a tablespoon of vanilla and placed the liquid in a bowl. She repeated this four times, moving her metal spoon slowly as if she feared she'd spill the precious liquid.

"What the hell are you doing, witch? Get on with it."

The young woman glared at Owen, and Izzy swore he flinched. "You said you wanted a binding love spell. This woman does not appear to be particularly willing, so I need to take my time to make sure it holds. You're welcome to leave, but I'm keeping my fee."

He snarled and narrowed his eyes. "Just do it."

A love spell? Was he kidding? Izzy could only hope this woman wasn't experienced enough to do a good job.

The witch nodded, pulled two long pieces of different colored yarn from her pocket, along with a pair of scissors and a six-inch ruler. She spent half a minute measuring the thread, and Chancellor shifted from side to side. A few times he looked out the window, as if he expected someone to come to her rescue. Izzy thought about saying something to hurry the witch along to prevent Chancellor from harming her further, but the longer this woman took, the better chance Rye had of rescuing her.

The witch placed both threads on the table in front of her. "Sir?"

Chancellor returned. "About fuckin' time."

"Please pick up one piece of thread with your left hand."

He huffed but obeyed. "Now what?"

"Repeat after me: Let this thread, unjoined and free, represent my woeful soul."

"That's crazy talk. My soul is not full of woe."

The witch stilled. "You paid me to make certain this woman falls in love with you. Now do it."

Her harsh tone shook Izzy, but the small boost of energy didn't last. She was finding it hard to keep her eyes open. Her strength was diminishing at an alarming rate. She needed help soon or she'd die, never to see Rye again. She sucked in a sob at that horrible thought.

"Fine." He said the words with much disgust. It was almost as if he believed Izzy's small cry was an expression of urging.

"Sir, I cannot guarantee success if your attitude does not improve."

"Fuck my attitude." He waved his gun. "Finish and be quick about it."

"As you wish." She lifted the other piece of yarn. "Take this in your right hand and repeat after me: Let this thread represent…" She glanced at Izzy. "I forgot your name, dear."

"Izzy."

"Her real name is Isadora Berta."

The witch shot her a glance, and her heart hammered. "Let this thread represent Isadora Berta. May she desire me and I her."

Chancellor mumbled the same response.

"Fine, now tie the two pieces of yarn together loosely and say: With this knot, may our souls be forever bound in endless love."

Her captor spit back the response. "Is that all?"

The witch nodded. Chancellor stepped behind her so she couldn't see what he was doing, but the metal clank implied he'd set down his gun. A few seconds later, he returned into her visual range, gun in hand.

The witch held out her palm. "Give me the yarn. In one hour, I will return it to you, and the spell will be cast."

"We don't have an hour."

Oh shit. What did that mean?

RYE PICKED THE first of the two names from the list that James had provided and then told Kalan to check the second house. Instead of using telepathy like he had the first time, he called his Beta using his cell. Whether it was atmospheric conditions or what, his connection with Izzy hadn't been all that clear, and Rye couldn't afford for Kalan to miss any instructions.

Ever since he received the names of the witches from James, Izzy's pain came at him in waves, stabbing at his soul. He could almost feel the life drain from her and willed Izzy to fight.

"What do you want me to do if I find Chancellor?" Kalan asked. "Wait for you?"

"Yes. If you find Izzy, call an ambulance stat then contact me. I'll join you, but don't wait to take him down if you think Izzy is in further danger."

"You do the same," Kalan said.

Being a deputy, Kalan had to act lawfully. Rye did not. Because the man had kidnapped Izzy, there would be hell to pay. Rye hadn't spent his youth developing his fighting skills for nothing. Knowing he'd be Alpha someday had kept him focused.

He'd already programmed the witch's address into his GPS, but the signal kept cutting out in the winding mountain roads, forcing him to drive around for a good fifteen minutes before he spotted a gray Toyota parked next to a grey double wide trailer that was in need of repair. When he checked the house number and found it matched the address, he pulled to a stop on the street at the end of the long drive, effectively blocking Chancellor's escape route. He then contacted his Beta. *"I found him."*

"I'll be right there."

"Call 911 for an ambulance."

"Will do."

It would be smarter to have the huge bear with him when he took down Izzy's stalker, but Rye wanted to tear Chancellor limb from limb all by himself—for stabbing him and for kidnapping Izzy. Kalan would merely arrest the son of a bitch, but Rye needed him dead.

He snatched his keys from the ignition. Not wanting to alert the occupants in the home, he didn't close his door. Two wolf scents emanated from inside, along with Izzy's. One was Chancellor and the other the witch Changeling.

Rye crept up to the east side window and peered in. Shit. Owen Chancellor was standing near Izzy with a gun in his hand. She was chained to the chair, her face was swollen on one side, and blood had stained her left shoulder. His blood pressure soared and his muscles tensed. *Motherfucker. You will die.*

Rye's teeth sharpened and his gut tightened. He wanted to rush in and shoot the bastard in the heart, but he didn't have a gun. Not wanting to be noticed looking in, he slid below the window, deciding his next move. Given the presence of his wolf signature, Rye was somewhat amazed that Chancellor hadn't come out to investigate. The odious man must be slipping or else he feared if he left Izzy alone, even for a few seconds, it might give her the upper hand.

Telepathing with Izzy now might give away his presence, so he blanked his mind. One thing was clear. He'd need to be in his human form to get through the front door. What he didn't know was whether that door was locked, but given the condition of the exterior, he bet he could kick it open with ease.

He also didn't know the magnitude of the witch's powers. Hell, if she could bind Izzy's abilities to do magic, what could this woman do to him? Stop him from shifting?

Maybe he should wait for Kalan, because no matter how good his tactical skills were, Rye was no match for a gun. If Chancellor shot him, he'd probably heal in a few days but by then, Izzy could be gone, and he could not let that happen. The only way to succeed would be to surprise the man.

The squeak of the outside door hinges signaled the front door had opened, and his pulse soared. Footsteps sounded on the wooden porch. Readying for the attack, Rye stepped out of his shoes and stripped off his clothes. He had to protect Izzy at all costs, and that meant killing Chancellor.

A heated argument ensued about the witch not finishing the job that she had been paid for, which gave Rye more time to prepare. Needing a visual, he slowly crept along the side of the building to see where Izzy was.

Once Rye shifted into his wolf form, Chancellor would for sure sense another wolf was near, but perhaps he wouldn't take the time to locate Rye's precise location.

"Help her," commanded the woman.

Rye's heart nearly burst. Feet pounded on the porch steps and then a car door opened. "Whose vehicle is that at the end of the drive? It's blocking me way," Chancellor whined.

Damn. Rye thought the winding driveway and dense trees would have hidden his SUV.

"It's my brother's. He's probably out back. I'll ask him to move it."

While Rye was totally confused why this woman would cover for him, he was glad she had. Perhaps she just wanted to get away from Owen and his lethal weapon.

Rye eased his way around the end of the trailer, just far enough to catch a glimpse of the gun trained on Izzy. Fearing he'd kill her, Rye charged.

Before he reached his target, Chancellor spun around and fired, but the shot missed. Remaining in his human form would put Chancellor at a distinct disadvantage. He must have realized that too, for a second later, Chancellor dropped the gun. Fur flew and bones cracked. Seconds later, Rye faced his nemesis.

Teeth bared and eyes glowing red, Chancellor came at him, but Rye had expected that move and managed to dart out of the way in time. Now behind Chancellor, Rye flung himself on the wolf's hindquarters and sunk his incisors into his flesh. The wolf yelped and twisted in an attempt to escape, but that only made the wound deeper. While Rye was pleased he'd taken the first bite, the injury wouldn't slow his nemesis down by much. The only way to kill this son of a bitch was to rip out his throat.

As much as Rye would have liked to prolong this wolf's death, he needed to tend to Izzy. The ambulance would be there shortly and having a dead man nearby with his throat ripped out would be hard to explain.

Crouching low, Rye waited for Chancellor to come at him again. Once the wolf's direction was set, Rye could make a slight change in his angle and go for the kill. Instead of the low attack Rye expected, Chancellor went high, his mouth aimed for Rye's neck.

Not going to happen today, buddy. Rye rolled onto his back then immediately leapt to his paws. Izzy's captor snarled. Before the wolf had the chance to regroup, Rye sprang with his claws extended and dug his nails into Chancellor's neck. Hanging on, he ripped and mangled the wolf's sinewy throat until blood spurted. Seconds later, Izzy's attacker fell to the ground, gasping for breath. Upon his death, the wolf shifted to his human form.

Rye immediately shifted back too, and using the water from the faucet on the side of the housed, he washed off the blood the best he could. He then quickly donned his jeans, shirt, and shoes. Not needing the paramedics to find the dead man, Rye dragged the body to a small copse of trees around the back of the house.

"Kalan, Owen's dead. I stashed his body to the west of the property under a maple tree. Take care of him for me." The last instruction wasn't needed, but Rye didn't want to leave anything to chance.

Sirens sounded in the distance, and he raced back to Izzy. She was half on, half off the back seat with her mouth open and her eyes mostly closed. Even with his excellent hearing and keen eyesight, he couldn't see her chest rise and fall or hear her breathing, but her life force still sent out a signal. Izzy was clinging to life—barely.

"Hold on, witchy woman. Help is on the way."

Chapter Nineteen

RYE PACED THE hospital waiting room, needing to hear that Izzy was out of surgery and doing well. When he'd found her in Chancellor's car, she had passed out from the loss of blood, but the paramedic had hooked her up to an IV and she'd roused. That didn't mean she was out of danger. It was too bad he couldn't donate some of his blood to help her heal quicker. If only she could shift, she'd be back to normal soon.

On his way to the hospital, Rye had called Izzy's parents and told them of the attack. They were understandably distressed, but fortunately did not ask a ton of questions. They said they'd be there shortly. He then called his dad, detailing what had gone down. He too wanted to come to the hospital to give him support. Of all people, his father understood the horrors that would result if Rye lost Izzy.

He'd just disconnected when Kalan telepathed, jarring Rye out of his reverie. *"I've taken care of everything. Chancellor had an unfortunate accident. His car went off the road at Gulver's Gap and bounced a few times before exploding. I called the department and reported the blaze. I doubt much will be left of him."*

That was brilliant. Burying the Changeling would have raised questions from his Scottish parents, as would taking him to the morgue since wolf attacks of the non-*Were* kind were rare. *"I didn't have a chance to clean up the blood. How will you explain that?"*

"When one of the deputies arrived to check out the scene of the

kidnapping, I told him that I had spoken with you right before the ambulance showed up. You told me that you and Chancellor had fought and that he'd been injured—hence the blood on the ground—but that he'd managed to escape. Due to the large volume of blood, I told him that much of it had to be Izzy's."

Rye had to hand it to his Beta. The man was a forward thinker. *"Thanks for having my back. I owe you a drink."*

"You owe me more than one!" Kalan laughed then sobered. *"How's Izzy?"*

"She's still in surgery." Several footsteps sounded causing Rye to turn around. *"Her parents are here. Talk to you later."*

"Keep me informed."

Mrs. Berta rushed up to him and threw her arms around him. He'd told them that Owen Chancellor was dead and that he'd killed him. Her mom leaned back and swiped a tear under her eye. Izzy's dad appeared stoic, while Missy's face was white. On her shoulder was a large bag that he suspected held some healing crystals and other assorted items.

Looking back on when he'd been stabbed, Rye doubted he could tell anyone what Izzy's sister had done to help heal him—other than it had worked.

"Any news?" her mom asked.

"Not yet. Let's sit."

Izzy's mother gripped his arm. "Did Izzy say anything about what happened?"

He shook his head. "No."

"You said this man had taken her to a witch. Did you speak with this woman?"

"I tried to find her after the ambulance left, but she had disappeared."

Missy pulled out a small burlap bag of something that smelled spicy, along with a round quartz ball. Closing her eyes, she held the objects and softly incanted. Rye figured it was her way of sending healing vibes to her wounded sister. It had worked for him and hopefully would for Izzy too.

A few minutes later, his whole family showed up, and he gave them the run down. Having everyone surround him helped with his nerves.

A long hour later, the surgeon appeared with his mask down at his throat. Rye's and Izzy's family jumped up.

"Izzy is fine. The bullet in her arm went right through, and the one to her hip missed the bone all together. She's one lucky lady."

"May we see her?" her mom asked.

"The nurse will let you know when she's out of recovery."

Hugs went all around. While Rye was Izzy's mate, her family needed to come first. There wouldn't be room for everyone. "You all see her first."

Her mom smiled. "Thank you, but don't stay away too long. I know my daughter will want to see you right away."

"You can't keep me away." Rye turned to Missy. "Keep doing your healing magic. We need her healthy."

Missy smiled. "I plan to."

With Izzy in good hands, Rye let her family keep watch for now.

His father clapped him on the back. "She's going to be fine, son."

"I know."

"We're going to head on out. We don't want to add any more stress to your mate."

"Appreciate it. I'm going to get cleaned up and come back when she's had a chance to rest."

He had plans to discuss with her—plans he hoped Izzy would agree to.

A week later

IZZY SWATTED AT Rye's hands. "I can do it myself." She picked up the plates from the dinner table and took them over to the sink to rinse them. This past week, he had tended to her wounds and hovered over her constantly until she'd wanted to scream. Sheesh. Rye treated her like she would break. Sure, she limped a little and had twinges in her upper arm, but she could function well enough.

Rye approached her from behind as she stacked two plates in the dishwasher, leaned over, and inhaled deeply. "Your scent is driving me crazy. I need you so much, Izzy."

While she had been ready to resume their relations, Rye had wanted to wait to make sure she was healed. Their exploits could get a little rough. She turned around. Before they engaged in sex tonight, she wanted to get something off her chest. "Not having sex has been super hard for me too, but I'm healed enough now." She held up a hand as he leaned in for a kiss. "We need to talk first."

He growled then kissed her, sending her hormones into high gear. Rye immediately sobered then broke the kiss. "The white moon is out tonight. Are you still deciding whether you want to learn to shift?"

She grabbed his hand and led him over to the sofa, dragging him down next to her. "No. I've made up my mind."

He brought her fingers to his lips and kissed each knuckle. "I'm good with whatever you decide."

She slipped her hands from his. "Thank you. I want to try. Once I successfully shift—assuming I even can—we won't know the extent or the speed of my loss. But you know what?"

"What?" He lifted a strand of her hair, brought it to his nose, and inhaled. "I love your smell."

She refused to be sidetracked. "I'm okay losing even half of my powers if it means I can always be a part of your life."

Rye drew her into a hug. "You will always be part of my life, but you don't have to make any sacrifices for me."

It wasn't a sacrifice. She sat back, trying to find the right words to explain it to him. "I am your mate, and to me that means being able to do the things you can—like run free in the woods with you."

Rye's eyes started to glow and the signs of shifting began. "It's rare that I have the chance to enjoy my other half. For me, being a wolf brings a lot of responsibility."

"Are you saying you don't want me to try to shift?"

He held up both palms. "Whoa. No. I want you to do what you want. I'd be thrilled and will help you, but if you change just for me, then eventually you'd be unhappy. I don't want to stand by and watch knowing you did it just for me."

Tears welled in her eyes. "But will you still love me if I can't part the sea or reduce a building to rubble with a flick of my hand?"

Rye cupped her face. "Now you are being silly. I will love you whether you can blow smoke up your ass, or shift at will. Your magic doesn't define you. Your caring nature, your love of family, and the way you see joy, is who you are."

She sniffled then laughed. "I can't blow smoke up my ass, only light it on fire—although I've actually never tried before."

He waved a hand while chuckling and kissed her forehead. "Whatever. Have you thought about our offspring? I'm assuming you want children?"

Rye's frown and worry lines made her want to rub them away. Their courtship had happened so fast that they hadn't taken the time to discuss these important issues. "I've thought about that a lot, and what their lives would be like whether they inherit my magic or your ability to shift, or both. Don't get me wrong, I love my magic, but at the same time, I hate it. You of all people know what it's like not to let others see the real you. If you shifted in the center of town there'd be an uproar."

His brows rose and he nodded. "Point taken. I guess that's why the Wendayans have their Cove and we have our lake." Rye dragged her onto his lap. "Listen. No one can foresee the future—okay, except for maybe Teagan—but we'll deal with whatever happens. When and if we decide to have kids, even if your magic is diminished, we'll love them for who they are. Hell, for all we know, your genes might cancel out mine. We could have human children."

She thought he was being a bit silly. "It's equally possible our children will inherit my old genes and your shifter genes."

"See? We don't know, and that's what makes life interesting. As long as we have each other, we can handle anything."

The tears streamed down her cheeks, but it wasn't from sadness. "You are a wonderful man. Did you know that?"

"It's easy to be when I'm around you."

At that moment, Izzy couldn't have loved him more.

"Did you mention something about being up for some wild, hard loving?" he asked.

"Why, yes I did."

He slid his arms under her butt and stood. She always marveled at his strength, and while she could have walked on her own, she loved being in his arms.

"I hope you are ready for a wild ride tonight," he telepathed.

"Trust me when I say I am going to test your control. As far as I'm concerned, it's no holds barred."

The door to his bedroom was ajar, so he backed into the room, and then set her down on the bed. "Take off your clothes so I can inspect your wounds."

She chuckled, knowing full well why he asked. "You know I'm almost healed. You just want to see me naked." She held out her right arm and wiggled her fingers. "Come here, you. I want to ply my sexual magic on you first."

He grinned. "Is that what you've been using this whole time? And here I thought you were just hot."

"You'll have to wait and see. Take your boots off. They're too hard to undo."

Rye obediently unlaced them and then tugged them off. "Now what?"

"How about closing your eyes? And don't cheat." Izzy wasn't sure he'd go along with her plan, but if his eyes were closed, there'd be fewer distractions—for her. She loved how his irises changed color as their lovemaking intensified. Too often she'd become mesmerized by the streaks of gold, brown, and swirls of green.

"What are you going to do?" He posed in what she called his

power stance—arms crossed and his gaze cast down at her.

Izzy worked hard not to laugh. "I'm not telling. You'll find out soon enough. Do you trust me?"

"With my life."

She smiled. "Then close your eyes."

"You drive a hard bargain, witchy woman." His eyes shut.

Izzy grabbed his waistband and drew him closer. "You'll be sorry if you open them."

His response was to laugh. The man seemed to find humor in most things—especially now that Owen Chancellor was dead.

She popped open the top button and then tugged hard, succeeding in undoing the rest of the fly. With her thumbs in his waistband, she lowered his jeans about three inches then stopped as soon as she realized he wasn't wearing any underwear. "You're missing something."

"Less work for you."

Smartass. His damn thick thighs made removing his jeans nearly impossible. "Can you help?"

With his lips pressed together, he stepped out of them, and the splendor of his cock nearly took her breath away. If she ever saw or spoke with Naliana again, she'd have to thank her for bringing the two of them together.

"You just going to stare, or are you going to touch it?"

Izzy glanced up, but his eyes were closed. "I wasn't even looking at you."

"Maybe not, but you were thinking about it."

He knew her too well. "For your information, I'm going to suck it dry."

Rye grabbed his cock. "Be careful. It's the only one I got."

She grinned and leaned over. With the lightest touch possible, she traced a path around the puckered rim of the tip. He growled, reached out, and grabbed a hunk of her hair. Ah, ha. The more time they spent making love, the better she was at understanding exactly what drove him crazy.

Giving him pleasure was her ultimate goal, which meant a delicate technique was needed so as not to excite him too much. She didn't want him shifting. Abandoning her brushing-tongue technique, Izzy drew him deep into her mouth. Pleasure flared.

"If I go off like a firecracker, it will be your fault," he ground out.

"You're stronger than that."

Rye grunted. "No man can withstand this kind of torture."

He was so good for her ego. *Better get used to it,* she telepathed.

With one hand, she stroked his dick, and with the other, she held him close. Loving his earthy flavor, she swirled her tongue as she bobbed her head up and down.

"If you keep it up, I won't be able to stop."

She didn't believe him. Izzy increased the pressure and pumped her fist faster. Rye tugged on her hair and stepped closer. A second later, he blew. Well damn.

Chapter Twenty

"**T**OLD YOU NOT to keep sucking on my dick like that."

Izzy was the first to admit that women were lucky to have the ability to climax time and time again, while men had to wait between releases—though Rye sure was super quick to recover. In fact, his cock was still hard.

He slipped off her sandals, undid her shorts, and tugged them off, taking her panties with them.

"Did you even look at them?" Izzy tossed him her best pout. "I put on leopard skin undies just for you."

His eyes glowed. "I notice everything about you. Does your bra match?"

"Take a look and see."

As if she was on fire, he lifted off her shirt, unclasped her bra, and flung it across the bed. "Nice."

"See if I wear sexy stuff for you anymore."

Rye dragged a finger down her cheek and her skin ignited. "I want the woman inside. I don't care what she's wearing or even if she has makeup on. Like I said before, it doesn't matter if you can turn into a turtle, a bear, or a wolf. As long as you're happy being with me, that's all that counts."

Once more, his words melted her. "I'm very happy, but I'll be even more so when I have that big cock of yours inside me."

He laughed. "And here I thought you were this shy, sheltered girl."

She clasped his head and pulled him close."

"What are you waiting for?" She sure did enjoy this telepathy thing. To hell with being able to send fire across her path or control water and air.

The kiss that followed would have knocked the proverbial socks off her had she been wearing any. They'd admitted how much they loved each other, and this time it wasn't under duress. The intensity of the kiss proved it. She explored as he probed. Only when they both needed air, did they break the kiss.

"You're looking mighty blue," he said.

"The bigger the ring, the more turned on I am."

"Then let's see if you can fill the room."

Izzy loved the way he thought. "Go ahead and try."

Rye slid between her legs, and when he captured a nipple and pulled it taut, she thought she'd shift. Power surged through her, forcing her to arch her back for more, and she wove her fingers through his hair and growled.

He glanced up then returned his attention to her other breast. Rye rolled to one side without breaking the connection and slipped a finger into her wet hole. With him out of hair-tugging reach, she dug her nails into his one shoulder and clawed the sheet with the other. "That's so intense," she said, her blue glow growing brighter.

Her comment seemed to urge him on. A second finger slipped in, and she almost came.

"Don't you dare climax on me," he commanded. "I want us to share this monumental event together."

Don't come? "Easy for you to say now that you're the one in control." As he wiggled his fingers back and forth, waves upon waves of erotic lust washed over her. "Lick me," she gasped.

Rye slid lower. Slower than the movement of glacial ice, he licked her long and hard. *"Feel good?"*

"Bastard."

Rye chuckled, but he didn't let up on the pressure. Nabbing one breast with his hand, he twisted the nipple, sending more spikes of bliss across her whole body. Between his tongue doing a dance on her clit and his fingers playing music on her tit, she was about to burst.

"Hurry!"

Hair had sprouted on his arms, and he seemed close to the edge himself. *"I will, but only because I want to make you happy."*

"How about, only because you're about to shift?"

He looked up, winked, and then scooted next to her before rolling onto his back. "Climb on and work your magic, my beautiful, witchy woman." Rye lifted his cock.

"You don't need to persuade me."

Izzy climbed on top. She was so wet it made Silver Lake look dry. Grabbing onto his dick, she guided his shaft to her opening. In an attempt to further excite him, along with herself, she only eased down partway. The friction on her inner walls, together with the change in his eyes made her lose control. When she tried to take in all of him, he'd managed to expand his cock, preventing her from encompassing his wide girth. Now who had the magic?

Widening her legs and leaning a little forward, she attempted once more to take him in. Rye clamped his fingers on her good hip. "I love how tight you are."

"It's because you're so big."

She had to wait until her inner walls stopped throbbing before she lifted off him. Once more poised above him, she leaned over to offer him her tits. Rye let go of her hip and latched onto both breasts. He pressed his face in between them while he pushed them together. Izzy slid down on his dick until he filled her to the hilt. Dear goddess in heaven.

Streaks of pleasure rippled in every direction as he stretched her to the max. She had to open her mouth to suck in more oxygen. "Kiss me."

Rye lifted his head and parted his lips. The second the kiss started, she lost all control. Her envelope of lust, passion, and love grew larger and larger until they were both cocooned inside. Their tongues collided and dueled as Rye took hold of her hip again and pounded into her. Her head swam, and her body heated. Lost in a vortex of pure desire, Izzy released her grasp on all she'd ever known and became one with him.

He broke the kiss, and then dragged his lips to her shoulder. The second his long incisors sunk into her neck, her climax descended and her bursts of light darted inside her blue globe. Flying higher than ever before, Rye's cock erupted and widened her passageway even more. She closed her eyes to absorb his essence and drink in all of his goodness.

With his arms wrapped around her back, he drew her close. Chest to chest, she allowed her muscles to give way and eventually slide into oblivion. At that moment, Izzy had never been happier. Sometime later, her blue glow finally dimmed.

He tapped her butt. "You want to go check out the moon?"

Izzy tried to lift her head, but it felt like it weighed twenty pounds. "Now?"

"Why not?"

She couldn't come up with a good reason. "If by some chance my powers were transferred to you during mating, I want to teach you how to do at least one thing, and tonight's as good as any."

"Really?" He rolled her onto her back then withdrew. "Let me clean us up."

He was back in a flash with a towel, and his enthusiasm helped spark her desire to go for it all. Both dressed quickly and were out the door before she realized they hadn't brought a flashlight. To her delight though, not only was the moon lighting their path, her eyes didn't have a problem seeing in the evening light.

Hand in hand, they walked on the path surrounding the lake, and then cut up through the trees toward the water's edge. She stopped in her tracks at the sight before her. With the moonlight glimmering off the water like silver ribbons swimming across the surface, it was more beautiful than ever before. No matter how many times she stood in front of the lake, she didn't think she'd ever tire of seeing its magnificence. "It's so incredible. I can see why your Clan chose to settle here."

"It has a magic of its own. Did you know the bottom is lined with pink quartz?"

That was the Wendayan's precious stone that had powers even she couldn't fathom. "I'd heard the rumor. Has anyone in town asked to mine it?"

"Not that I know of, but I doubt they understand its value." He squeezed her hand. "Let's head on over to my rock and see if you can teach an old dog a new trick."

Izzy leaned against Rye. She loved his humor and his need for adventure. "I've never taught anyone before. From what I've been told, either you have the magic or you don't."

"If our mating didn't transfer your magic to me, I'm okay with that."

He was being such a good sport. "Let me see what you can do before I attempt to shift. It's possible any abilities you've received might disappear along with mine."

Rye wrapped his arms around her. "Stop worrying about it. As long as I'm with you, I'm good. To have it even for one night would be a thrill."

"What would happen if you ever lost your ability to shift?"

He was silent for a moment. "That's a tough one. I imagine my parents wouldn't be too happy, as I would no longer be fit to be the Alpha, but I'll deal with whatever the consequences may be. Gotta take chances if you want to gain something."

She kissed him. "When did you become so wise?"

"When I met you."

Joy and love filled her. "Okay, let's give this a try." Izzy picked up his hand and folded his fingers in the same manner her father had taught her. "It might be better if we face the water."

He chuckled. "So we don't set the forest on fire?"

"Yes." Izzy demonstrated her technique and explained how she shot fire out of her palm. "Be sure to close the fingers slowly in order to improve your aim. Now you try it."

He glanced over at her, and then up at the moon. "Here goes, but don't laugh if I can't do this."

"Never." She probably couldn't shift either.

Rye held out his hand, and when he closed his fingers, a spark flew out and fluttered a few feet before extinguishing. "Did you see that?" He acted like a kid at Christmas.

"Yes. It means you can do it. Curve your fingers a little more and concentrate on the heat and color of the flame."

Rye inhaled and tried again. This time the flame shot out about a foot. "That's fantastic." He faced her. "I'm going to practice every night until I get better."

"I hope you can. I honestly have no idea what you'll be capable of. Want to see if you can create a water spout?"

"Fuck, yeah."

Once more, she instructed him, but after several tries all Rye could do was make small ripples across the water. "It's a start," she said sensing his disappointment.

He lifted her up and swung her around. "I don't care if I never improve. I was able to experience what made you who you are. If I can do nothing tomorrow at least I had it once."

Her eyes watered at his sentiment. "Aw. That's so sweet. Tell me what I need to do to shift."

"Are you sure?"

She'd never been surer of anything in her life. "Yes."

"Okay then. I've never had to teach anyone either, but I remember what my father told me. He said to envision my inner wolf, and once I've connected with it to start running. Your vision will turn black, but only for a moment. Your bones will crack and the first time you shift, you'll think you're being pulled apart, but don't worry, it gets easier the next time."

"How do I turn back?"

"Just think of your human self and it will happen."

If it didn't work, she'd really be in trouble. "I guess I need to get naked, right?"

Rye approached and placed his hands on her shoulders. "Yes, but be thankful I'm in a generous mood."

"What does that mean?" From the cheer in his voice, she could guess.

"Once you're naked, I'll want to mate with you again."

Izzy punched him in the chest with her uninjured arm. "You're lucky I don't create a tornado while I still can and send your ass into the middle of the lake."

He laughed. "Don't worry. I'll be good. I know how much this means to you."

They both undressed and placed their clothes at the base of the rock. "So I just think about the wolf inside me and start running?" she asked.

Bones cracked and fur flew. Two seconds later, Rye was in his wolf form. His paws landed on her hips, and then he took off. Izzy followed. At first, she had to hold her tits to keep them from bouncing. She lasered her focus on Rye and how wonderful it would be to become a wolf. No sooner had that thought entered her head than pain overtook her entire body. Her vision blurred then turned a dark gray, but somehow she could still see through the fog. It was like she was directing a movie where she had the starring role.

Before her mind could wrap itself around the whole concept of becoming an animal, she was inches from the ground. Holy hell. She did it! Rye howled.

"*Follow me,*" he telepathed.

Good goddess. They could communicate even in wolf form. Totally free for the first time in her life, Izzy took off after Rye. He leapt onto a rock and she jumped up after him as if she'd been a wolf her whole life. He darted down the other side then zigzagged around the trees. The pine floor was sweeter than she ever remembered and the air cleaner. All of her senses appeared to have tripled in intensity.

Rye returned to the lake and waited for her. All of a sudden, he shifted into his human form, and Izzy wanted to do the same. He'd said to picture it, and the shift would happen. Suddenly, her bones stretched and cracked. Disoriented for a moment, she suddenly was back, and relief poured through her.

"Well?" he asked.

"I have no words other than amazing, fantastic, exhilarating."

Rye lifted her up, stepped closer to the water, and tossed her into the lake. The cold shocked more than chilled her. "Why did you do that?" she asked after surfacing.

He laughed. "Initiation ceremony."

"I'll show you an initiation." Hoping she still had her powers, she formed a wind tunnel around Rye and drew him toward her, totally ignoring his protests. She then lifted up the funnel, moved it over the lake, and when she let go, he sunk like a rock.

When he didn't surface, her pulse raced even though she didn't sense he was in danger. Izzy swam toward the drop location, and suddenly, a hand yanked on her ankle and pulled her underwater.

Rye's face appeared inches from her. He grabbed her by the waist and shot them to the surface. His lips found hers, and their kiss under the white moon was one to remember.

He broke the contact. "Let's swim ashore and change."

When they reached land, Rye hopped out onto firm ground and held out his hands. Without thinking, she gave him both of hers and he tugged her to her feet. Whoa. The pain in her arm was gone. She rubbed the area on her shoulder where she'd been shot but could barely feel anything.

"Your wolf healed you in case you're wondering," he said.

Only then did it occur to her that when she was in her wolf form, she'd been able to run without a limp. "That's incredible."

"What's incredible was that I was able to fulfill my childhood dream of becoming a dragon. I'll overlook the fact that fire didn't come out of my mouth."

Rye led her back to the rock where they donned their clothes with some difficulty. Putting them on over a damp body sucked.

Out of nowhere, two sets of hands clapped and she stilled. Izzy spun around and her knees weakened. "Naliana?"

Chapter Twenty-One

I T HAD BEEN a long time since Rye had seen Naliana, and he wasn't sure what to make of her sudden appearance. James was with her, standing tall, his salt and pepper hair newly trimmed. His wide grin made his eyes crinkle, but it was the extra sparkle in them that had James looking even younger.

Naliana stepped closer. Her long white hair glowed in the moonlight, and the gauze dress she wore made her appear a bit too thin.

"I see you two have mated." She clapped once more. "I'm so happy for you."

Izzy glanced over at Rye and then at Naliana. "Did you have something to do with getting us together?"

Naliana clasped a hand over her heart. "I'm not a pretend goddess. You know how much I believe in true love." She placed a peck on James's cheek. Light glinted off his smile as he wrapped an arm around her waist.

"Is that why you called me home?" Izzy asked. "So I'd be with Rye?"

"That was one of the reasons."

Now the goddess had piqued Rye's curiosity. "You didn't send Owen Chancellor after Izzy just so I'd have to protect her, did you?" Damn, he hadn't meant to sound accusatory, but if that was what Naliana instigated, then the goddess that everyone looked up to wasn't who everyone believed her to be.

"No, Rye! When I realized what that horrid little toad of a

werewolf was planning to do, I had to warn Izzy. I didn't want her in the same continent as him. I had no idea he would follow her to America or that he planned to kidnap her."

The tension in his body dissipated. "I appreciate that."

"I did, however, have Izzy do your aura cleansing instead of Kathryn."

"So Mom was in on it," she telepathed to Rye.

"Remind me to give her a big hug."

"What did that stalker creep really want?" Izzy asked. "When he kidnapped me, he had a witch try and perform a love spell."

"Owen Chancellor wanted to bring home a bride to make his parents proud, mostly because he was such a big disappointment to them. When he saw your magic, he decided you'd be perfect."

James held up his hand. "Just so you know, the witch wasn't really going to do a love spell, Izzy. She was stalling for time until Rye arrived."

"How do you know this?" Rye asked. Once more, his tone came out sharp.

James shifted his weight. "She's kind of working for me."

Rye was confused. First, Naliana admitted she was aware of what that man had planned for Izzy and had done nothing to stop him. Now, he learned that James had a Changeling working for him. Growling, Rye asked, "Care to explain?"

"Easy there, big fellow. I told you I have sources in the Changeling world."

James only said that he had sources, but he'd never mentioned anything about them being Changelings. "And?"

"She's one of them. In fact, Olivia is in the process of coming over to our side."

He'd like to know how that was even possible, but he doubted he'd receive a satisfactory explanation.

"Are you sure?" Rye asked. "Wasn't she the same witch who put a spell-binding on Izzy?"

James waved a hand. "No. That witch was *conveniently* unavailable when Chancellor tried to contact her again. He was redirected, shall we say, to Olivia."

His powers and connections were quite extensive and remarkable. Rye had probably learned all he could today.

The lovebirds' time was very limited. Not only did Naliana and James have a lot of catching up to do since she'd be returning to the heavens tomorrow, Rye needed to ask Izzy something.

Naliana lifted Izzy's hand. "You made the right choice by shifting and wanting to share your life with the man you love. For your sacrifice, I can reveal to you that your powers will diminish over time, but never completely. They shall remain at half strength."

Izzy looked up at him, smiled, and then returned her gaze to Naliana. "Thank you."

She let go of Izzy's hand and once again kissed James on the cheek. "I made a sacrifice for James, and I've never regretted it." She looked over at Rye. "As for you, sir, your shifting abilities will remain strong, and those talents you've received from Izzy will continue to intensify, but not so much to interfere with your destiny—that of being an Alpha to your Clan."

"I thank you two for everything."

"We won't keep you two any longer," James said. "We just wanted to stop in and congratulate you."

For the first time in his life, Rye was at a loss for words.

Like a puff of smoke, the two trailed off into nothingness.

He faced Izzy. "Can you believe that?"

She laughed. "I'm just as stunned as you are, but I'm happy that we have their blessings."

He didn't care if the goddess and James were in favor of their mating or not. Rye was in love and content for the first time in his life.

"What I find interesting is that the witch was working with James." He snapped his fingers. "That was why James didn't hurry when I pounded on his door and told him you'd been kidnapped. He knew. He was stalling until Chancellor arrived with you at that woman's house. I'll be damned."

Izzy wrapped her arms around him. "I'm just glad James was able to help."

"Me too." Rye inhaled as he slipped his hand inside his pocket and rubbed his finger around the smooth pink quartz band. "There's something I want to give you."

"What's that?"

Being a wolf, he really wasn't sure how this human proposal stuff was supposed to work. "In our Clan, once I've bitten you and you've accepted my offering, we are mated for life."

"I know."

His heart pounded. "I realize that humans do things differently than us, so I want to respect your tradition." He withdrew the ring from his pocket and lifted her left hand. "I want all the humans to know that we are together. I'm also willing to have a human style wedding ceremony if you want. What do you say?"

When he slipped the ring onto her fourth finger, she sucked in an audible breath. "Are you asking to marry me?"

"I suppose I am, but I didn't do a good job of proposing, did I?"

She threw her arms around him. "It was wonderful. I don't need a fancy wedding. I'm happy being your mate and doing things your way. If you think about it, I'm not even totally human anymore."

She was part shifter. "I know, and I couldn't be happier, but your parents might like to see their girl walk down the aisle in a beautiful white dress, and that is absolutely fine by me."

"They just might. I'll let you know."

"You bet." He kissed her like he never had before, and his cock responded as usual. He ended the kiss. "We probably ought to head back. I think we've had enough excitement for one night."

She smiled. "I'm sure we can conjure up a bit more if we really try."

"You might be right." He did love his mate.

THE PAST WEEK had been hectic preparing for the Alpha ceremony. He'd been busy practicing and helping his parents and the Murdochs set up the tables and chairs. Rye was definitely ready for the passing of the title. Because the temperatures late in the day were still warm, they held the ceremony outside on the extensive acreage connecting the Murdoch and the McKinnon properties. A few of the Clan members had built a makeshift stage and erected a stand with a hanging curtain behind it.

His dad approached him. "You ready for this big step, son?" It was hard to hear over the noise coming from the boisterous crowd. As far as Rye could tell, every bear and wolf shifter living in or near Silver Lake had come to the ceremony.

Rye chuckled. "A little late to be asking now, don't you think?"

His dad patted him on the back. "You'll do just fine. With Izzy by your side, the two of you will be excellent leaders. Why if it hadn't been for your mom, I would have made a lot more mistakes in my time as Alpha. Izzy seems like she's very level-headed."

"She is." Rye glanced over at Kalan who was nervously shifting his weight. His sister and brother were standing next to him, while his parents were helping Rye's Mom place the food on the massive buffet. Nearly every shifter family had contributed to the feast.

Rye glanced around for Izzy and spotted her with her mom. "You have your spare pair of jeans, right?" he asked his dad. None of the bears or wolves had an issue walking around naked since they frequently shifted, but Rye didn't want to embarrass Izzy's parents.

"Yes son. Now are you ready to get this show on the road?"

He nodded. His dad motioned to Devon who then walked up to the stage and whistled. The crowd immediately settled down. Rye was thrilled his brother had been able to make it tonight. If anything ever happened to Rye, Devon would become the next Alpha.

"Would everyone please stand?" Devon asked. "We are about to begin the transfer of leadership."

Whether wolf or bear, this event would only happen once or twice in their lifetime. Daniel Murdoch, Kalan's dad, stepped up onto the stage and Kalan joined him, facing his father. Rye's dad stepped next to Daniel, and Rye followed suit, standing next to his best friend and Beta-to-be. He glanced over at Kalan whose back was so straight he looked like his spine might crack from the pressure.

"Smile. You and I are going to rock this leadership stuff," Rye telepathed.

His shoulders sagged slightly. *"We are."*

Cameron McKinnon held up a hand. "Thank you for coming to this ceremony. For years, you all have welcomed me and my family, along with Daniel and his. We've had some struggles, but by working together, we have overcome many obstacles. I am confident that my son, Ryerson, and his Beta, Kalan, will be even better leaders than we were. With Isadora Berta, a Wendayan, by my son's side, Silver Lake will be even more united."

The crowd applauded and pride swelled. When the clapping subsided, his father continued. "I know all of you will offer the same respect to these young men as you have given to Daniel and me, so it is with great pleasure that I hand over my leadership role as Alpha to my son Ryerson."

As choreographed, both Rye and his dad shifted into their wolf form, as did Daniel and Kalan Murdoch into their bear form. While his father had told him what would happen, Rye was in awe when his father actually knelt in front of him with his head bowed, and then both Murdoch men followed suit. Rye howled to signify he agreed to be the group's Alpha.

The crowd cheered, and then all four animals jumped off the stage and ducked behind the curtain before shifting. If Izzy's parents hadn't been in the crowd, they never would have gone to such lengths. Once they changed, they headed back out where the crowd was still clapping.

"Congratulations, son." His dad hugged him. "Go, get 'em. They're in your hands now."

"I'll do my best."

Daniel Murdoch embraced his son then shook Rye's hand. His

father looked over at Rye's arm. "It's official son. The gods have agreed."

His pulse soared when he saw what had once been just a paw print on his tribal band, was now a wolf's head; and his father's wolf head imprint had transformed into just a paw print. "I'll be damned."

Kalan lifted his sleeve. "Holy shit," he whispered. His grin said it all. His bear paw was now the head of a roaring bear.

The two of them hugged. Rye then looked around for Izzy and motioned her over.

"Me?" she telepathed.

"I can't rule without you—or should I say, I don't want to."

Izzy worked her way through the crowd, and when she came to his side, he just had to kiss her. He wanted every person to know that he'd found the perfect mate.

Epilogue

T EAGAN POMPLEY FINISHED changing the linens on the massage table, set out the oils, and then lit the incense to prepare for the next customer. Suddenly, she swayed and had to grab onto the table or chance falling. Her vision blurred and her stomach churned. An image of Elana Stanley surrounded in darkness swept across her mind's eye.

Then everything cleared and Teagan's balance returned. She hopped up onto the table to gather her wits. That had to have been the quickest premonition she'd ever had, which meant something bad was about to happen to Elana in the future.

I hope you enjoyed Izzy and Rye's story. To keep up-to-date on my releases, sign up for my newsletter:
http://eepurl.com/U1dm1

Next up is Elana and Kalan's story—Catching Her Bear. Below is the first chapter!

Chapter One

BROTHER JACOB STOOD behind the hand carved table on the raised platform and shut the lid to his laptop. He then held up his hand to quiet the Changeling Council members sitting on unforgiving wooden chairs before him. The dim lights flickering from the six gas sconces barely illuminated their faces, and the black wool curtains covering the cement walls added the air of mystery and secrecy. He glanced at the two new additions to the room that he'd personally commissioned. They were two statues, the bottom half of which was human, but from the shoulders up they were pure wolf. The eyes made of red onyx were lit from behind to make the eyes glow.

He glanced around. Three of the members had failed to don their robes. They would suffer for that slight.

Once the ten-member group stilled, he addressed them in his most Alpha tone. "Brother Chris, tell us that you've procured the sardonyx."

This blood colored stone, when imbued with a powerful curse on the red moon, could extract the powers from a Wendayan. The Changelings could dominate all of Silver Lake and beyond if they were able to harness the witches' magic.

"Not yet, Brother Jacob. The Stanleys claim the Indian mine where they'd found the stone in the past has closed, but that they are scouring the earth for another one. It's difficult to find the red stone suited to our exacting needs."

Jacob slammed his hand on the table and the sound reverberated. "Unacceptable! Tell them they have one week or they die." He didn't bother wiping the spittle from his chin.

"Yes, Brother Jacob."

KALAN MURDOCH, THE werebear Beta to the clan of wolves and bears, sat in his Alpha's living room, pad of paper in hand, discussing their duties as newly appointment leaders in Silver Lake, Tennessee. Even at ten in the morning, his eyes were tired from taking notes, and the strong coffee Rye's mate had made for them didn't seem to be working.

Right after Rye's mate, Izzy, had moved in, she'd placed a lamp next to the lounge chair, but even that didn't provide enough light. He did appreciate the added crystals, colorful candles in all shapes and sizes, and some much needed throw pillows, like the one supporting his back.

Kalan pointed his pen at Rye. "Here's a thought. We could exact enough pink quartz from the bottom of the lake to give a piece to everyone." The recent rash of robberies and fires had alarmed some of the members, and the quartz would provide a modicum of protection against the evil and ever illusive Changelings. Personally, he'd never use the stuff, but rumor had it that power resided in the quartz.

Ryerson McKinnon, his Alpha, propped his feet on his wooden coffee table. "It's not like it's their Kryptonite. Only the massive amount of the stone at the bottom of Silver Lake seems to temporarily drain the Changelings' powers when they enter our land."

That made sense. "Do you think something the size of Izzy's quartz crystals would have an effect on one of them?" He bet if a Changeling ever walked into this room, he'd feel his powers drain immediately.

"Not really, which is why we need to get closer to them and find out what they're up to. Stop them before they can do more damage. You're the cop. There has to be something you can do."

"Not without attracting attention." The sheriff wasn't even aware shifters exist, so he wouldn't be getting any support from the department. "Perhaps James can help."

James, their resident immortal and husband to the moon goddess, Naliana, had a Changeling contact who had helped them locate Izzy when that Scottish Changeling Owen Chancellor had captured Rye's mate.

"I don't want to rely on him for everything," Rye said.

"Asking for help a few times isn't exactly relying on him. If you don't want to go that route, what do you propose?" Kalan asked.

"Not sure. Izzy might have been joking at the time, but she suggested we find someone to go undercover to infiltrate their ranks."

Kalan laughed. "Right. That would be a death sentence."

"Not if we hire an out-of-towner, someone who has experience working undercover."

"Good luck finding him. Our kind doesn't exactly advertise in the Yellow Pages."

"I can be patient." Rye leaned forward, snatched his cup off the table, and tipped it back. "Did I mention Izzy's birthday is in two days, and that we're going to have a little get together here this weekend?"

Kalan had to assume the discussion about how to handle the Changelings was now closed so he tossed his pad on the lounge at his feet. "No. Then again, you've been a bit preoccupied."

His best friend grinned. "I'm telling you, having Izzy in my life has been the best thing that has ever happened to me."

Kalan could tell where this conversation was going, and he needed to nip it in the bud. "I'm happy the two of you are mated, but just so you know, I'm perfectly content being single." As a deputy and part time detective in the criminal division of the sheriff's department, he worked erratic hours. Sampling the women of Silver Lake whenever the need arose worked perfectly for his lifestyle. More importantly, now that he was the new Beta of the large clan of wolf and bear shifters, he didn't need to be tied down to one woman. "What can I bring to the party?"

"Nothing. I'm barbequing some burgers and stuff. I think Izzy's mom and sister are doing the rest."

Kalan wasn't the type to arrive empty-handed. He'd at least buy Izzy a gift. Easing off the lounge chair, he grabbed his empty coffee cup and walked it over to the kitchen and set it in the sink. "Gotta get back to work." Before taking a step, his cell rang and he checked the caller ID. "Speak of the devil."

Rye stood. "Go ahead and answer it. If our paths don't cross beforehand, I'll see you Saturday."

"You got it."

As Kalan left Rye's, he answered his phone. "Murdoch."

"It's Phil." Phil Smythe was his boss and the head of the Criminal Division.

"I was just on my way in," Kalan said.

While the day was overcast, the warm summer air was scented with the sweet aroma of pine from the surrounding forest.

"Good, but first I need you to run down a lead. It's regarding the Donaldson warehouse fire. We brought in the owner and he claims he was at a church social that night." Phil gave him the lowdown.

"I'll check it out."

Kalan hopped in his freshly washed Jeep and headed into town. As he passed the colorfully painted Bloom's of Hope flower shop, located across the street from where Izzy worked, an idea popped into his head. He'd check out the lead then buy Izzy a birthday bouquet. It seemed like a safe gift. Women liked flowers. Surely it would stay fresh for two days.

A mile out of town, Kalan parked in front of the white wooden church that was graced with a tall, beautiful spire. From the outside, it looked pious as hell, especially with the stone statue garden off to the side that included the heavenly family and a host of other saints. He'd always wondered if he hadn't met a real goddess what his belief system might have been. Now wasn't the time, however, to debate the validity of religion.

He eased out of his Jeep. Not wanting to be disrespectful, he drew back his wavy locks and secured it with a rubber band then headed inside. His eyes quickly adjusted to the low light, most of which was coming from the beautiful stained glass window above the altar. Kalan inhaled the rich scent of fresh furniture polish and let his muscles relax.

He had to admit the cushions on the wooden pews made it rather homey. No one was inside praying, or whatever a person did inside a church, but he had to believe the pastor was around somewhere.

Thinking the door off to the side of the rather austere altar might house some offices. Kalan went in search of the man, passing a series of religious photos on the wall. He located him at the end of the hallway.

The door to his office sat ajar and a man wearing glasses and a buttoned down shirt was at his desk. Kalan knocked and entered. "Excuse me." He held up his badge.

The pastor slipped off his glasses and set them down, shoved back his chair, and then stood. "Yes, officer. How may I help you?"

"I want to ask you about one of your parishioners, a Jack Donaldson."

"What about him?" His tone, along with slightly pinched lips implied he was ready to defend the man at any cost.

"I need to know whether he was at your church social on the 23rd of this month."

"He most certainly was. In fact, I spoke with him about his daughter."

"What time was that?"

The pastor ran a hand over his chin. "I can't say when our conversation occurred exactly, but the social ran from six to nine, and Jack Donaldson was there the whole time. He's such a wonderful man. Never misses church."

Well, that was a bust. The fire department said the blaze had been set around seven. Not that Kalan thought the pastor would lie, but he wanted to touch base with a few others to be thorough. "Do you have a list of the guests who attended?"

"They all signed in. If you give me a moment, I'll make you a copy."

"That would be great. Thanks."

The pastor pulled open a desk drawer and extracted a book. He then made a copy on his scanner and printed it. "Here you go."

Jeez. It was three pages of names. "Appreciate it."

"Any time. Say, I haven't seen you in church."

"Been busy." Kalan didn't need to be discussing his habits and waved the papers. "Best be going. Thanks again."

"Come again soon, son."

Kalan didn't respond. He glanced down at the papers again and hoped one of these names could provide a lead. Because most of these folks would be at work for another few hours, he decided to purchase the flowers for Izzy then head into the station.

As he drove closer to the Blooms of Hope flower shop, a parking space freed up in front, which he considered good karma. As Kalan passed the display window, he slowed, spotting the perfect gift for Izzy. It was a vase of pink, red, white, and orange wild flowers behind a cute stuffed wolf. Izzy and her wild, magical ways would love it. That was easiest present he'd ever found.

When he stepped inside the fragrant smelling shop, that ease he'd just experienced totally disappeared. His heart fluttered and his incisors lengthened. Holy shit. He didn't detect a shifter close by, so there was no need for his body to go into fight mode. Something was seriously wrong.

A girl about twenty, with her hair in a braid and more tattoos on her arm that there were flowers in the shop, stood behind the counter placing pink roses in a long box for a customer. Nothing about that should have triggered his unwanted reaction. A large glass cooler filled with flowers of every kind lined one wall, but as a bear shifter, he wasn't allergic to anything related to the outdoors, so he shouldn't be feeling light-headed.

The clerk packaging the flowers for the customer turned her

head toward the back. "Elana, customer."

Elana, Elana. He mentally snapped his fingers. Izzy's friend was named Elana. When he was at the Emergency room the day Rye had been injured, he'd also had a strange feeling that he couldn't identify. He recalled his only thought was that he had to get out of the waiting room. Hell, he'd been so flustered he'd walked right into the closed glass door.

"Hello," Elana said stepping out from the back, her voice like a smooth malt whiskey.

Dark hair with hints of red lay loose around her shoulders. This time she'd let it hang loose instead of pulling it back in a ponytail, and boy what a different that made. Her soft, blue eyes looked dreamy, almost as if she'd been sniffing too many flowers and had gotten high.

His heart nearly stopped when his gaze lowered to her perfect pink lips, the exact shade as the rose petals her assistant was stuffing into the cardboard box. As he let his eyes roam from her eyes to her chest to her legs and back up to her face, his nails began to grow and totally freaked him out. What the hell was wrong with him? She was a mere human.

But what man or rather shifter could resist drinking her in? The top of her head was no higher than his chest, and if he took a guess, her tits were probably a D cup, enough to fill his big hands. And her lush hips? Man they were made to cradle a man in ecstasy. Where the hell did those thoughts come from?

Say something, you oaf. "Hey there. I, ah, heard you gave Rye a lift back from the Emergency Room. That was really nice of you. I would have driven him but I was called back to work." *Babble, babble.*

Not only that, it was bull and totally lame. He didn't even receive or make a call when he was there.

"I did. How is he?"

"Healed up great." She'd know if she'd spoken with Izzy. However, her friend might not have told her Rye's wolf helped him heal quickly.

Kalan might have elaborated, but every word in his head seemed to have evaporated. Even concentrating took effort. *Focus*. He couldn't. Something was happening to him that scared the shift out of him. Kalan Murdock was always in control—unless he was in the presence of Elana it seemed.

"Are you here for some flowers?"

"Flowers? Yes. I saw a wild flower display in the window along with a stuffed wolf that would make a perfect gift."

She smiled, but her eyes didn't light up. In fact, she appeared to be in pain. For the life of him, he couldn't think of what he'd said to make her so sad.

"I'll make one up for you."

He wanted to say he'd take the one in the window as that would hurry things along, but when she rushed over to the flower cooler, he didn't want to make things worse for her. As soon as the first customer left the store, the girl working the register stepped into the back. Alone with Elana, his senses heightened. Kalan placed a hand to his forehead thinking he might be coming down with something.

Elana brought the fresh flowers and vase to the counter and began to arrange them. Mesmerized by her agility and care, Kalan slowly lifted his gaze to her face. While not classically beautiful, Elana Stanley was a striking woman who made his libido pound with unwanted desire—or at least it was unwanted at this moment.

"Here's the wolf," the girl from back said waving the stuffed animal. "You want me to ring him up, Elana?"

Her smile seemed to wobble. "Sure."

It then hit him like a stampede of wild boar. "You're friends with Izzy. Do you think she'll like this for her birthday?"

As if the sun peaked out from the clouds, she grinned. "Absolutely. In fact, a while ago she was admiring one like it in the window."

Relieved he'd picked something his Alpha's mate might like, he withdrew his credit card and handed it to tattooed girl at the counter.

"Are you going to Izzy's birthday party?" he asked. She was Izzy's best friend, so it made sense she would be.

"Yes. You?"

He had come in for a present, but he could always say he'd purchased the gift because he wasn't able to make it. "I'm hoping to. I work long hours and I get called into work all the time."

He didn't want Elana to think he was looking to hook up. Given she was his Izzy's best friend, he wouldn't even chance asking her out, not even to the movies. It could only end in disaster.

She set the bouquet and wolf on the counter. "Here you go. We're open Saturday until noon. If you stop in, I'll give you a helium balloon to attach to the vase."

Elana was too nice. "If I have time."

Kalan couldn't wait to leave. He was battling this unwanted attraction again, and if he shifted in a public place, the world would never be the same. As soon as he signed his name, he swiped the vase of flowers and wolf off the counter and rushed out. As he reached the door, the wolf slipped from his fingers and dropped on the floor. Damn. He swore Elana giggled.

Face heating, he bent down, retrieved the gift, and hurried out. No way in hell, he was going to that party and subject himself to being near her again.

PACK WARS (Paranormal)
Training Their Mate (book 1)
Claiming Their Mate (book 2)
Rescuing Their Virgin Mate (book 3)
Box Set (books 1-3)
Loving Their Vixen Mate (book 4)
Fighting For Their Mate (book 5)
Enticing Their Mate (book 6)

MONTANA PROMISES (Full length contemporary)
Promises of Mercy (book 1)
Foundations For Three (book 2)
Montana Fire (book 3)
Hart To Hart (book 4)
Burning Seduction (book 5)
Montana Promises Box Set (books 1-3)

ROCK HARD, MONTANA (contemporary novellas)
Montana Desire (book 1)
Awakening Passions (book 2)

HIDDEN HILLS SHIFTERS (Paranormal)
An Unexpected Diversion (book 1) – FREE
Bare Instincts (book 2)
Shifting Destinies (book 3)
Embracing Fate (book 4)
Promises Unbroken (book 5)

SOUTHERN SHIFTERS KINDLE WORLDS
Bear 'N Dirty

WERES & WITCHES OF SILVER LAKE
A Magical Shift (book 1)
Catching Her Bear (book 2)
A Surge of Magic (book 3)

Author Bio

Want a FREE book? Sign up for my newsletter and receive MONTANA DESIRE.

COPY AND PASTE INTO YOUR BROWSER:
http://eepurl.com/U1dm1

Check out my latest interview on You Tube:
youtube.com/watch?v=sQo5pyyVMDI

Not only do I love to read, write, and dream, I'm an extrovert. I enjoy being around people and am always trying to understand what makes them tick. Not only must my books have a happily ever after, I need characters I can relate to. My men are wonderful, dynamic, smart, strong, and the best lovers in the world (of course).

You'll find me most days on my chaise lounge with my laptop and my iced tea(unsweetened!) on the side table. I love to sleep in late and write into the wee hours. I also love FB, so you'll find me on there, too!

I believe I am the luckiest woman. I do what I love and I have a wonderful, supportive husband, who happens to be hot!

Fun facts about me

(1) I'm a math nerd who loves spreadsheets. Give me numbers and I'll find a pattern.

(2) I'm addicted to taking pictures (I taught high school photo for 30 years). I plan to periodically post some of my favorites on my newsletter [so sign up!].

(3) I also like to exercise. Yes, I know I'm odd. Not only do I walk with different women each week, I teach Pilates twice a week at a local rec center, and lift weights the other days.

I love hearing from readers either on FB or via email (hint, hint).

Social Media Sites

Website:
www.velladay.com

FB:
www.facebook.com/vella.day.90

Twitter:
@velladay4

Gmail:
velladayauthor@gmail.com

Google:
plus.google.com/u/0/116041077486216602121/posts

Tsu:
www.tsu.co/velladay